PRAISE FOR *BEST BAB*

"A clever twist on an old favorite, *Best B...* ... humor and attitude. A must-read fo...

—MELISSA DE LA CRUZ, #1 *NEW YORK TIMES BEST-SELLING AUTHOR*

"A glitter-dusted story about ambition, revenge, forgiveness, and friendship. Add to cart!"

—LISI HARRISON, *NEW YORK TIMES* **BEST-SELLING AUTHOR OF** *THE CLIQUE*

"Hilarious, fresh, and fun! *Best Babysitters Ever* is the best! A great homage to a classic series with plenty of modern moxie."

—MICOL OSTOW, BEST-SELLING AUTHOR OF *MEAN GIRLS: A NOVEL*

"From the start of this debut novel, Cala flexes her prodigious comedic muscles, managing to render the three friends both as sympathetic heroines and as the victims of lives more humorous than they would like. . . . They may never get another babysitting gig, but you're hooked on their story for life."

—*NEW YORK TIMES BOOK REVIEW*

"In her middle grade debut, Cala artfully uses humorous banter to paint the dissimilar friends' realistic relationships as well as their bumbling efforts to vocalize their feelings and advocate for themselves. . . . An appealing, humor-filled update to a classic series."

—*PUBLISHERS WEEKLY*

"Thanks to witty banter, ample humor, and excellent characterization, readers will enjoy following this group of young dreamers as they attempt to gain some independence in their preteen lives." **—***KIRKUS REVIEWS*

"A breezy, entertaining read, this book and the promised sequels seem likely to fill a role similar to the original—as reading material kids choose for themselves." **—***HORN BOOK*

"Fans of the Baby-Sitters Club books are a natural fit for this debut novel about three enterprising girls. . . . Cala incorporates themes of sibling rivalry, jealousy, competition, friendship, manipulation, entrepreneurship, and first crushes into this realistic series starter."

—*BOOKLIST*

"Even readers who have never had the pleasure of hanging out with the BC girls of yore will find Malia, Bree, and Dot all likable in their distinct ways, and they'll appreciate the book's mix of snark and heart." **—***THE BULLETIN*

PRAISE FOR *THE GOOD, THE BAD, AND THE BOSSY*

"This smart, humorous tale should inspire girls to dream big, experiment, and problem-solve through challenges." **—***KIRKUS REVIEWS*

"This light, amusing installment features relatable characters who are imperfect yet well meaning." **—***SCHOOL LIBRARY JOURNAL*

Best ~~BAD~~ Ever
BABYSITTERS
MISS IMPOSSIBLE

Best ~~BAD~~ BABYSITTERS Ever

MISS IMPOSSIBLE

CAROLINE CALA

Houghton Mifflin Harcourt

Boston New York

hmhbooks.com

Produced by Alloy Entertainment

30 Hudson Yards, 22nd FL
New York, NY 10001
alloyentertainment.com

The text was set in Garamond.
Book design by Opal Roengchai

The Library of Congress has cataloged the hardcover edition as follows:
Names: Cala, Caroline, author. Title: Miss Impossible / Caroline Cala.
Description: Boston : Houghton Mifflin Harcourt, [2020] | Series: Best babysitters ever ; 3 | Audience: Ages 10 to 12. | Audience: Grades 4–6. |
Summary: Malia, Dot, and Bree get a much older—and scarier—client than they expected, but looks can be deceiving.
Identifiers: LCCN 2019045780
Subjects: CYAC: Babysitters—Fiction. | Clubs—Fiction. | Moneymaking projects—Fiction. | Best friends—Fiction. | Friendship—Fiction. | Humorous stories.
Classification: LCC PZ7.1.C27 Mi 2020 | DDC [Fic]—dc23
LC record available at https://lccn.loc.gov/2019045780

ISBN: 978-1-328-85091-1 paper over board
ISBN: 978-0-358-54767-9 paperback

Manufactured in the United States of America
1 2021
4500824809

For my parents

CHAPTER ONE

MALIA

Sometimes, thought thirteen-year-old Malia Twiggs, it was easy to take stuff for granted. Like the sun, for example. It was so warm and bright, just shining in the sky. But it was always there, so it was easy to forget how lovely it was. Or free time. Or friends. Or snacks. Or crushes. When you had these things, you kind of expected they would always be there. Until something happened that made you put everything into perspective.

Indeed, the world was full of wonderful things everyone was too distracted to notice. Which was why Malia was trying to appreciate absolutely everything.

Just a few months ago, Malia had been an entirely different person. Back then, she had been a regular kid—with zero responsibilities and lots of free time to do things like stare at her crush's Instagram feed while being very careful not to accidentally like anything.

Then, one fateful October day, she and her two best friends, Dot and Bree, founded Best Babysitters. From that point forward, Malia became CEO of their joint business, which meant she was responsible for the vision and direction of the company. Or, as she liked to think of it, it meant she was in charge. After figuring out how to successfully watch children and then how to maybe even have a good time doing it, Best Babysitters had brought on three employees. This turned out to be a terrible idea for approximately four gazillion reasons, including the part where their new hires tried to take over their jobs, their clients, their crushes, and their dignity. At the same time, Malia got roped into an internship by her evil big sister, Chelsea, working for Ramona Abernathy, a retired tech mogul who lived in their town.

Having multiple jobs was a lot like when your favorite teacher was out for a while and you got stuck with a mean substitute, or when you came down with a cold and thought longingly of all the nights when you had failed to notice how nice it was to be able to breathe through both nostrils as you were falling asleep. Malia had learned a lot at her internship

—mostly corporate vocabulary words and how to juggle multiple jobs at a time—but was all too relieved to be free when it was over.

She was happy to go back to being just a CEO again. With all this newfound freedom, Malia was ready to take Best Babysitters to extraordinary new heights. She had plans to grow the company, win more clients, and offer extra services.

Today, though, there was just one new client to attend to. Baby steps.

"So how old is this kid?" asked Dot Marino, one of Malia's best friends and fellow babysitters.

"The mother didn't say." Malia shrugged. "She was very withholding with details. All I know is that it's an only child, and her mother seems to think this could become a regular gig."

"Well, I hope this kid is nice," said Bree Robinson, the third best friend rounding out Best Babysitters. "Or at least not trouble."

Malia, Dot, and Bree were making their way to this latest job, following the directions on Malia's phone. That was pretty much all the information they had, as the client had offered few other details about what they were getting themselves into.

Even after everything Malia had been through, the first

day watching a new client was always a bit like the first day of school, a mix of excitement and uncertainty. It was a new beginning, filled with fears and possibilities.

They approached the home, a two-story house with pale yellow siding. Wind chimes tinkled in the breeze, while underfoot, a welcome mat read, *Shut the front door!*

Dot rang the doorbell. Malia glanced around, taking in the small front porch, the gray front door, and the matching mailbox.

"Why do I feel like I've been here before?" Malia asked.

Had one of her mom's friends lived here or something? She knew she hadn't been here recently, but there was something distinctly familiar about this place.

The door opened.

Malia's heart dropped. Bree gasped. Dot's mouth formed a surprised *O*.

All three babysitters stood blinking in disbelief.

None other than Zelda Hooper—the biggest bully in Playa del Mar—peered back at them from inside the front hallway. The meanest of the mean girls, Zelda was known for all kinds of pranks—spreading rumors, writing mean notes, leaving weird and unwelcome surprises in her victims' lockers. Just last week, she had somehow gotten ahold of the boys' soccer team's giant jug of Gatorade and laced it with hot sauce. In fifth grade, she had swapped out the letters on the big sign in front of the school to announce that Max Featherson peed himself. On the regular. Back in elementary school, she was legendary for hiding bugs — huge, terrifying bugs — in people's backpacks and storage cubbies.

Her face was always twisted into a constant look of anger, and today was no exception. Her auburn hair hung in shiny curtains that fell past her shoulders. Her wide-set green eyes sat atop her small, slightly upturned nose. Malia had seen that face all too often in the halls at school, and also in her nightmares. She certainly hadn't expected to see it here, at her job.

Malia now realized why the house seemed so familiar. She had been here before, in what felt like another lifetime. Way back when they were classmates at Playa del Preschool, Malia and Zelda had been friends. At least, Malia had thought they were friends, until Zelda turned on her.

A full moment passed, and no one knew what to say.

"What are you weirdos doing here?" Zelda finally asked.

"Uh, your mom called us," Malia supplied.

"For babysitting," Dot added.

"Are we sure we're at the right house?" Bree asked, glancing at the number on the house like perhaps it had changed. "Do you have a younger sibling or something?"

Zelda's face twisted into a grimace. Just as she was about to respond, her mother—a mom-aged carbon copy of Zelda —appeared behind her. Her outfit seemed better suited for the pages of a fashion magazine, or maybe a red carpet event. She wore a silver blouse with billowy sleeves and simple black pants. But her silver platform sandals were what really stole the show. Malia remembered being mesmerized by Zelda's mom's clothing as a kid. No matter how many times she and Zelda had asked, they were never allowed to play dress-up with her mother's precious things.

"Girls! How lovely to see you!" she trilled, causing Malia to wonder how any person with a mom as sweet as Zelda's could ever turn out as mean as Zelda. "Please, come in."

They trudged across the welcome mat and through the front door. Inside, the house was warm and friendly, with brightly colored patterned carpets. Floor-to-ceiling shelves were filled to the brim with books and artifacts, and family photos lined the walls. It smelled like fresh-baked chocolate chip cookies. If the home hadn't belonged to Zelda, Malia would have wanted to move in.

"I just made some cookies," Zelda's mom said, confirming what their noses already suspected. "You should feel free to help yourselves. It's so nice to have a homemade after-school snack, don't you think?"

How was it possible that such an evil person came from such a lovely place? This felt like the set of a sitcom, while Zelda's actions suggested she came from a cave.

"Please make yourselves at home," Zelda's mom continued. "Watch TV or a movie or do whatever you like. Zelda obviously knows where everything is!"

Zelda, arms crossed, remained silent.

"Uh-huh . . ." Malia trailed off, still unsure what was going on here. Were they seriously babysitting Zelda Hooper right now? Their own peer?

"Of course, don't hesitate to call me if you need anything, okay?" Zelda's mom gave a sheepish smile as she backed up toward the front door. "But most important, have fun!"

And with that optimistic urging, she was gone.

"Well! This is weird," said Dot, stating the obvious.

Zelda did not speak.

"What should we do?" Bree asked.

"Eat cookies?" Dot offered. She was never one to pass up baked goods, especially when they were fresh.

"What are you in the mood for, Zelda?" Malia ventured. She figured the least she could do in this awkward situation was be polite.

Zelda crossed her arms over her chest. "I'm in the mood for you not to be here."

"Um . . . okay. Then why are we here?" Malia asked.

"My mom felt sorry for you and your stupid business and I guess she wanted to give you something to do," Zelda said matter-of-factly.

"What? Why?" Malia couldn't believe what she was hearing. Why would Zelda's mom feel sorry for them? They were good at their jobs and they had plenty of business. "I mean, that's nice of her and all, but our business is doing great."

"First of all, you're thirteen. You don't have a 'business.' You have a hobby. And you must not be *that* busy, because three of you are currently babysitting one person. Who doesn't need babysitting in the first place."

Malia started to respond, but Zelda held up a hand. "Look, this whole setup wasn't my idea, and obviously, I want no part of this. But here you are in my living room. So my advice is to stay out of my way." For emphasis, Zelda made an ugly monster face, rolling her eyes and sticking out her tongue like a grimacing Halloween mask.

The girls blinked at one another in silence. This day was definitely not going in a direction anyone could have predicted. They were suddenly trapped in a home with a person they typically went out of their way to avoid, and they had no choice but to stick it out. A job was a job. Even this job.

"So, did you want to watch a movie?" Bree tried.

"I'm sorry," Zelda glanced around the room. "Did I hear something?" She continued looking for the source of the phantom sound, like Bree didn't exist.

"I just thought . . . like, a movie doesn't mean we have to talk to each other or anything . . ."

Zelda rolled her green eyes. "Do you remember the time I filled all the Girl Scout cookie boxes with live grasshoppers?"

The girls nervously nodded. Of course they remembered. How could anyone ever forget?

"Good. So here's how this afternoon is going to go. I'm going to go to my room, where you're not invited. I'm not going to talk to you, and you're not going to talk to me. And if you fools tell anyone at school about this, the grasshopper incident is going to look fun compared to what I will do to you." And with that, she stalked off through the house and slammed her bedroom door.

The girls didn't have to question the threat; everyone knew she meant it.

For the rest of the afternoon, the girls cowered in the kitchen, nibbling cookies, never daring to speak above a whisper. There were a few silent Zelda sightings, which were a bit like catching a glimpse of a Sasquatch — brief, terrifying, hard to explain. Every time she appeared, the girls were on edge. But true to her word, Zelda refused to interact with them.

By the time Zelda's mom appeared in the front hall, they couldn't get out of there fast enough.

"Did you girls have a fun afternoon?" she asked.

"Oh, yes!" said Malia, with a bit too much gusto.

"Terribly fun," added Dot.

Bree, who was pretty much incapable of lying, just nodded.

"I'm so glad." Zelda's mom smiled sweetly, apparently unbothered by the fact that her daughter was nowhere to be seen. "Thank you so much for your time." She handed Malia a stack of bills, which made the last few hours seem somewhat worth it.

"Thanks for the cookies!" Malia said, pocketing the cash and making a beeline for the front door. The girls shuffled wordlessly out the door and down the Hoopers' front path.

"Well, that'll go down as the weirdest job ever," Malia said as soon as they were safely to the sidewalk. "I thought little kids were bad, but teenagers are the *worst*."

CHAPTER TWO

Dot

After the kerfuffle at Zelda's house, they couldn't wait to get back to the business of watching actual children. Their last job had reminded them just how enjoyable an energetic, imaginative, easily bribable toddler could be. Today, they were watching the sweet, predictable Gregory kids — four-year-old Jonah and six-year-old twins Piper and Plum.

The second they arrived on the property, Malia dashed across the Gregorys' front yard, trying to get a glimpse of the house next door, which was occupied by the family of one Connor Kelly. Dot wondered if Malia would ever get over her ridiculous crush on Connor. But if the last few years were any indication, she supposed Malia wouldn't.

"What are you doing?" Bree asked.

"Oh, just seeing if anything is new in the neighborhood!"

"By which you mean, seeing if anything is new in Connor Kelly's backyard?" Dot corrected.

"Shhhhh!" Malia said, looking around dramatically, like a secret agent on a mission.

"If he's not outside, then I doubt he can hear us," Dot said. "Also, it might be good if he heard. Don't you want something to happen, already? We cannot go on this way forever."

"Speak for yourself!" Malia whispered. She tiptoed up to the fence and crouched down on all fours so she could peer through a space in the hedges that lined the Kellys' fence.

"Oh, that's stealthy," said Dot. "I'm not allowed to say his name, but it's totally cool to crawl around on the ground outside his house."

Malia stood up, a look of dismay on her face. "It doesn't matter. I can't see anything," she reported. "Not even a glimpse of anyone in the windows." She bounded back to join her friends on the front steps.

A moment later, the door swung open to reveal a girl who looked about their age. She had hair the color of caramel that fell in artfully tousled waves, as though she had just gone running on the beach for approximately eight minutes. She wore a red-and-white-striped tee, half tucked in, that perfectly matched her neat, manicured red nails. Dot didn't recognize her from school. In fact, she was quite certain she had never seen her before. There was something about this girl, but Dot couldn't quite put her finger on it. She had a certain . . . je ne sais quoi. (Which was French for a hard-to-explain magical quality that kind of means "something extra.")

"Hello?" said the girl, though it sounded more like *Ahh-lo?* "How can I help you?"

"Hi there, we're here for babysitting," said Bree.

"Yes, I am the babysitter," said the girl, which came out sounding like *zee baby-sitter.* She definitely had an accent.

"No, we are the babysitters," said Malia, pointing to herself.

"*Oui. Je suis la baby-sitter,*" said the girl, emphatically.

"I feel like perhaps we aren't getting through here," said Dot.

The girl shot her a pointed look, like Dot had said something that was both unbelievably stupid and offensive. Dot was momentarily taken aback. Who did this girl think she was?

"Don't worry, Genevieve!" said Mrs. Gregory, rushing to the door. "You go back to the kids, I'll take care of this."

Genevieve sashayed away as Mrs. Gregory offered Malia a pained smile.

What in the universe was going on here?

"I'm so sorry, girls. We're having a bit of a chaotic day today and I must have completely blanked on calling you to cancel," Mrs. Gregory explained. Dot and Malia exchanged glances. *Cancel?* "That's our new au pair, Genevieve. Her family just moved here from Paris! She's going to be watching the kids from now on, while helping them learn valuable language skills."

"I see," said Malia slowly.

Mrs. Gregory regarded them warmly.

"We've so appreciated your services, but we thought it would be good for the kids to experience something different, you know, culturally." She smiled.

The sound of children singing a French song drifted softly from the living room. The three Gregory kids sounded like little cherubs forming a chorus in the clouds. *What was this?*

"Oh! That sounds so nice," said Bree.

"A very worthy investment," Dot agreed, nodding.

"Well, I guess we'll be going, then," said Malia.

"We'll be sure to call you in the event that Genevieve is unavailable!" Mrs. Gregory said, giving them a little wave before closing the front door behind her. The girls stood on the step for a moment, processing what had just happened.

Dot sniffed the air like a hound. "Is it just me, or does it smell like baguette?" she asked. Dot was a big fan of baguettes. She would know that smell anywhere.

"You're imagining things," Malia said.

"No, it does smell kind of like bread." Bree sniffed. "Or maybe croissants?"

"Yes, and it's making me hungry," Dot said. Because it totally was.

"You guys," Malia grumbled. "That is absurd. It cannot be. There is no way that girl is inside baking French bread products in addition to teaching the kids how to count and sing like some sort of small French angels. She looks like she's our age. There's just no way."

But anyone with a working nose would have to admit the air outside the Gregory house did smell suspiciously delicious.

"Bread products aside, should we be worried about what just happened?" Dot screwed her face up. "Do we think this is going to spiral into another Seaside Sitters situation?".

"Not that again," Bree wailed.

She was referring to the time when Malia's evil older sister, Chelsea, had started her own rival babysitting organization and nearly put them out of business. In the end, though, Best Babysitters had prevailed.

"No. Seaside was a whole organization," Malia said confidently. "This is just some French girl who's new to town and trying to earn some extra cash."

"With perfectly tousled hair," added Bree.

"And an apparent talent for baking," Dot chimed in.

"Whatever. I'm sure this is just some weird phase," Malia continued, almost like she was trying to convince herself. "Like, remember when the Seaside Sitters were teaching everyone Dutch?"

"*Ja*," said Dot, then laughed at her own joke.

"That lasted for about five minutes, and this will be the same. The kids will probably never go for it. They're going to miss us, and our inside jokes, and our silly games. Just wait. This will never last."

"I'm sure you're right," said Bree, though she didn't sound convinced.

"This is just one girl, who was hired by one family," Malia said. "It's nothing to be concerned about."

"*Ja!*" Bree agreed.

"*Très,*" Malia added, in a very strong French accent. "*Très, très ridicule.*" She paused for a moment, lightly nibbling on her thumbnail. "But maybe we should make some calls, you know, just in case. To confirm that everyone is still on board for their regularly scheduled jobs this week. Once we talk to everyone, we'll know there's no reason to worry."

Bree nodded.

Dot knew better. Malia's whole "casual thing" was all an act, and she was probably freaking out inside.

First, they called the home of the Larsson triplets—Ruckus, Thor, and Bronson—who lived with their two moms in a giant house on a bluff overlooking the ocean. Though they had initially gotten off to a rough start with the family due to a failed babysitting job that had resulted in a priceless sculpture being broken, the Larssons had since become one of their most dependable clients. The moms, Dina and Erika, paid super-high rates and had the most impressive snack cabinet on the planet.

Malia put her phone on speaker so everyone could hear the conversation.

"Malia!" said Dina Larsson, after just one ring. "It's so nice to hear from you."

Surely this was a good sign.

"It's so funny you called," Mrs. Larsson continued, before Malia could even get a word in. "Because I've been meaning to give you girls a shout today. I don't quite know how to tell you this, but as it turns out, Erika and I have decided to try something new for the boys."

Malia frowned. The corners of her mouth turned so low, she looked like a frowny emoji.

"We've hired a French au pair. You know how valuable language skills are, so it was an opportunity we simply couldn't pass up," Dina explained.

"Riiiiiight," Malia said, slowly. She looked like she was trying hard to keep her cool. "We totally get it. But please know we're always available if you change your mind."

"Well, that was unexpected," Malia said as soon as she hung up.

"Don't freak out, don't freak out, don't freak out," said Bree, as Malia scrolled through her contacts to make the next call. Dot couldn't tell who Bree was trying to soothe—Malia or herself.

Next they called Mrs. Woo, Ruby and Jemima's mom, who reported that the Woo girls were also enthusiastic new students of French. Even their favorite client, Aloysius Blatt, a child genius who surely didn't need the likes of a French tutor, had also gone to the dark side. Even one of their very last resorts

—spending extra time helping to babysit Bree's siblings—yielded terrible results, as Bree's family had hired a new French "helper" to come to their home a few afternoons a week.

"I can't believe it!" Bree cried. "This is worse than the time they went out to celebrate my birthday and accidentally left me at home."

Malia nodded solemnly. "At least that was an accident," she agreed. "This just feels like betrayal."

It turned out that there were three French sisters—Genevieve, Sophie, and Claire—and they were all babysitters. Motivated, hireable babysitters. With presumably perfect hair.

"Whoa," said Malia, as they trudged slowly down the sidewalk into their suddenly free afternoon. "I don't even know what to say."

"I can't believe we've lost all our jobs to French au pairs!" said Dot. "I mean, really, what is the appeal?"

"We were wrong," Bree said, worry coloring her voice. "This is worse than Seaside Sitters. Like, way worse."

"Also, can you believe the way Genevieve looked at us?" Dot grumbled.

"Like what?" asked Bree.

"The way she *squinted* at me! Like we were a bunch of unfashionable basics!" Dot huffed. "I also half tuck in my shirts!

I also artfully tousle my hair! I speak French that is kind of okay! Like, not full sentences really, but I understand a bunch of words. And I also know how to mind children." She didn't like feeling less-than, and this French sitter had gotten under her skin.

"Yes, and you are good at pretty much everything," Malia said. "It's not a contest. There are some sitters who can teach some kids a different language. So what? That does not make them better."

"But it *does* make them hired," Bree said.

Malia wasn't having it. "No. We bring just as much value to the Playa del Mar babysitting market as any au pair."

"I agree," said Dot. "But if the parents are dazzled by these fabulous newcomers, we're out of luck."

"Then maybe we just need to work on our image!" said Malia. "You're the director of marketing. Why don't you brainstorm some ideas?"

Right now, Dot's only idea was to stay as far away from this as she possibly could. She didn't like the situation one bit—not just because they had lost the Gregory job, but also because it had made her feel bad. Malia might be one to go marching into the flames, but that wasn't her style.

One thing was clear: This wasn't good.

CHAPTER THREE

Bree

I don't feel better yet!" yelled Bree, as she turned a corner.

"Me neither," Malia chimed in.

"When are the en-dolphins going to start working?" Bree asked.

"Endorphins," Dot corrected her. "Keep going, they're bound to kick in soon."

After the news broke about the French au pairs, Dot had suggested a bike ride to help cheer them up. And get their endorphins going. Or something like that. They had biked all over town, and Bree still felt pretty low. Now they were almost at their final destination: the gazebo at the end of the cul-de-sac.

As they reached the intersection, a tiny green creature darted out into the street right in front of them.

"What IS that?" Malia called.

It looked sort of like a frog and sort of like a newt. Bree recognized it at once.

"Salamander!" Bree yelled, slamming on her brakes. "Watch out!"

Bree steeled herself for impact. The salamander narrowly missed getting squished by the bike's tires. It continued running in its funny way, then looked around, like it had gotten lost. Run, run, look. Run, run, look.

"Be careful!" Bree called after it. The salamander didn't acknowledge her one way or another.

"Close call," Dot said.

"I know!" Bree exclaimed. "I can't believe I almost hurt it!"

Salamanders were a tiny species of amphibian that sometimes frolicked in Bree's family's backyard. Just a few weeks ago, when her mom was gardening, one of them popped out of a bed of daisies when her mom wasn't expecting it and run right across her foot. Her mother had been so surprised and frightened, she'd thrown her trowel in the air and run straight into the house. To this very day, the little shovel was still there, exactly where her mom had left it.

Bree didn't think salamanders were scary. She thought they were cute. And she was really glad she hadn't run one over.

They continued down the road, everyone biking a bit more carefully this time. That is, until an absurd commotion erupted from a nearby bush.

"ROARRRRRRRR!!!!!!!" The bush rustled as an earsplitting noise rang out.

"What the—" Bree knew better than to take her eyes off the road, yet she couldn't help but look over at what appeared to be an actual dinosaur emerging from the shrubbery lining the stretch of highway. It was short (for a dinosaur), but still taller than a person.

The girls were so focused on the dinosaur, they didn't notice the tiny stampede of salamanders that had wandered into the street.

"YOU GUYYYYYYS!" Bree called, as their bikes careened directly into the salamander traffic.

"Oh my god!" Malia exclaimed, bringing her bike up short. "I think I squished its tail!"

"You WHAT?" Bree shrieked. She couldn't stand the thought of a poor, defenseless animal suffering because of a bicycle.

"The tails grow back!" Dot called.

"Huh?" Malia hopped off her bike.

"Salamanders have the distinction of being the only amphibian that can regenerate body parts!" Dot said. "So you don't have to feel bad!"

"But doesn't it hurt in the meantime?!" The thought was still too much for Bree to handle.

"ROARRRRRRR!!!!" said the dinosaur again.

Bree looked over just as the dinosaur collapsed onto the ground, where it appeared to be deflating. The sound of laughter erupted from within the bushes, and three small figures climbed out.

Dot snorted.

"Ugh!" said Malia. "I should have known."

"YOU THOUGHT IT WAS A REAL DINOSAUR WE TRICKED YOU THAT WAS THE BEST!" yelled a tiny, angry boy. Bree recognized him as Smith Morris, a boy who lived on the cul-de-sac.

Chase, Clark, and Smith Morris were three inseparable brothers whose first names all sounded like last names. They were incredibly close in age — Chase and Clark were five-year-old twins and Smith was just eleven months older — and the three of them were always, always together. They had more energy than a hornet on Red Bull and more aggression than a Tasmanian devil that had been wronged. They were skilled climbers, occasional biters, and amateur but determined pranksters. In short, they were every babysitter's nightmare.

Ever since they'd begun the club, the girls had made a pact to avoid watching them, at any cost.

"MWAHAHA!" Smith yelled at the top of his lungs, running around the girls like an imp. "I'M GOING TO SQUASH ALL THE SALAMANDERS!"

"Yes!" yelled Chase, putting his fist in the air.

"You will do no such thing!" Bree hollered back.

"What color are salamander guts?" asked Clark.

"I BET THEY'RE GREEN AND BLACK AND YELLOW!" screamed Smith.

"Let's find out!" said Chase.

"If you try to hit a salamander, I'm going to turn you in to the police," said Dot.

"YOU CAN'T DO THAT!" yelled Smith.

"Yes, we can!" Malia argued. "For animal cruelty."

Bree noticed a salamander standing near the curb, looking at her with what she could swear was a look of concern.

"Don't worry, salamander," she said. "We'll protect you."

It cocked its head a little, then scurried off.

Could salamanders even hear? Bree wondered. Did they

have ears? She wasn't sure. She realized there was an awful lot she didn't know about salamanders, including why they seemed so intent on crossing this one particular stretch of street. But she was determined to find out.

Later that night, Bree settled onto the family room couch with her laptop, ready to do some lizard-themed research. Veronica, her hairless sphynx cat, curled up on a blanket next to her, prepared to nap until someone offered him dinner. Bree's nine-year-old brother, Bailey, was sprawled on the floor in front of them, playing a driving video game.

"Salamanders in Playa del Mar," Bree recited, as she typed it into the search engine. She was greeted with a wide array of salamander facts and photos.

"Look, Veronica, aren't they cute?" Bree asked, pointing to her screen. There were so many types of salamanders, and Bree thought all of them were adorable. They were slick and scaly and a little bit wrinkly in places, sort of like Veronica.

Veronica—named after Veronica, a pop star so famous no last name was necessary—opened his huge yellow eyes and gently pawed at the screen.

"I know, I like the spotted one, too." Bree patted Veronica's wrinkly head.

In recent days, Bree had gotten much better at offering encouragement, thanks to Dr. Puffin, Veronica's cat therapist. After weeks of dedicated therapy sessions, Bree now understood that when Veronica did something good—like snuggling up next to her or actually pooping in his litter box as opposed to any number of potted plants scattered throughout the house—she was meant to offer lots of positive reinforcement, to encourage more of the same behavior. The more Bree praised him, the more pleased Veronica seemed that his efforts were not in vain. Truth be told, cat parenting wasn't all that different from babysitting.

Of course, many of Veronica's behavioral improvements were due to the fact that Bree had recently had a major breakthrough. After many feline outbursts (and more destroyed objects than she cared to remember), Bree had discovered that Veronica hated glitter (which was sad, as glitter was formerly Bree's favorite color). The mere sight of anything sparkly was enough to drive Veronica over the edge, or at the very least, encourage him to shred the offending item.

Since the breakthrough, Bree had needed to make some major life changes. Her decor, her school projects, and especially her wardrobe had become decidedly less flashy. She could get away with the occasional metallic, if it was something small, like nail polish. But full-on glitter was a thing of the past. If she was really being honest, Bree had to admit that she missed shiny things.

But no matter—Veronica was worth it. He was her beloved, wrinkly, hairless cat-baby, which no amount of glitter could ever compete with. And looking on the bright side, the situation had forced Bree to open herself up to a whole new world of self-expression—filled with neon colors, loud prints, and mixed patterns. The world was her brightly colored oyster.

Bree gave Veronica one last pet, then settled in to read about salamanders. She learned that a newt was always a salamander, but a salamander was not always a newt. She learned that a salamander is a type of amphibian with a long tail in its adulthood. She learned that salamanders also go by the names spring lizard, water dog, and mud puppy. Last but not least, she learned that salamanders like to stay cool, which means they often avoid the sunlight. This explained why they'd been crossing the street in the evening, when it was especially easy to get hit by rush-hour traffic.

"Oh my goodness!" Bree exclaimed.

"What?" asked Bailey, who was completely engrossed in running other drivers off the virtual track.

"Did you know that every year, the salamanders of Playa del Mar migrate across the same stretch of Waveland Avenue?"

"No," Bailey said, never taking his attention off his animated race car. "I don't think I even know what that means."

"IT MEANS THAT INNOCENT LIZARDS ARE DYING," Bree shrieked. "AND SOMETHING MUST BE DONE!" Her tone caused the napping Veronica to stir.

"Look what you made me do!" Bailey grumbled, throwing down his controller. "You scared me, and my car just got completely trampled by these other cars!"

"That's exactly what's happening to the salamanders!" Bree said, hoping this might help prove her point. "The salamanders are trying to cross the street, and they're getting squished! Right here in our own town. And we need to help them."

"You're so weird," said Bailey, shaking his head as he left the room.

Bree followed him into the kitchen, where she found her stepdad, Marc, massaging some kale at the counter.

"The salamanders are getting squished!" she repeated for this slightly larger audience. Perhaps an adult would care.

"The who?" said Marc.

"The salamanders," Bailey said, rolling his eyes. "Bree is obsessed."

"Is that like a band you kids are into?" Marc asked, concentrating on a large, dark green leaf.

"No! It's a type of amphibian that's partial to shady, leafy, aquatic habitats!" Bree said, repeating what she had just learned.

"Oh! You mean, like, actual salamanders," Marc said. "So wait, why are they getting squished?"

"I'm so glad you asked!" Bree knew an adult would care. "You see, it's currently their migratory season. They're typically nocturnal, and often travel at night, when it's cooler. But this also means it's dark, so it's harder to see them. They move slowly, and they need to cross the street. And they keep walking across the same part of Waveland Avenue, where they're in danger of getting run over."

"Oh," said Marc, twisting his mouth up in a strange sort of grimace. He seemed confused about whatever it was he had just learned. Perhaps he did not care after all.

"Bailey, do you know the difference between a salamander and a newt?" Bree asked.

"No, and I don't care," said Bailey, ever the honest one.

"It's a trick question! A newt is a type of salamander," Bree answered, anyway. "And salamanders are often referred to as lizards, but they are actually technically amphibians."

"NOOOOOT!" yelled her two-year-old half-sister, Olivia, bopping around in her booster seat. "NOOOOT!"

"Also, did you know that some salamanders have teeth, and some don't?" Nobody answered, so Bree kept going. "Kind of like how Olivia didn't have teeth for a while!"

"TEEF!" yelled Olivia. "TEEF, TEEF! I HAVE TEEF! NOOOT HAVE TEEF!"

Olivia wasn't yet much of a conversationalist, but at least Bree could always count on Olivia to pay attention to her. It was more than she could say about the rest of her family.

"Well, salamanders are dying right here in Playa del Mar, and I'm going to do something about it!" Bree announced. She felt triumphant, the way she had previously assumed people only felt in movies. But unlike in the movies, nobody cheered or pumped their fist in the air and yelled. Instead, Bailey grabbed a box of Cheez-Its off the counter as Olivia threw her sippy cup on the floor. Marc gave a distracted smile, then turned back to the kale.

No matter. Innocent creatures were suffering. There were salamanders in need of saving, and Bree had work to do.

CHAPTER FOUR

MALIA

It was time for their weekly Best Babysitters board meeting, and as far as Malia was concerned, it wasn't a moment too soon. They had very important matters to discuss — their business had nearly dried up since the appearance of the French au pairs and something drastic needed to happen. And also, less urgently, they had snacks to eat.

"Where's Bree?" asked Dot, upon her arrival in Malia's bedroom. "I thought I was late."

"Who knows?" Malia shrugged. "But she better get here soon. Time is of the essence."

"Is she bringing the animal?"

Before Malia could answer, the sound of shuffling cascaded down the hall. Moments later, Bree, dressed in red pants and a green shirt with pink horses printed all over it, came crashing through the doorway. It was a lot of look, not to mention a particularly dramatic entrance, even for her.

"Sorry I'm late!" Bree trilled, looking around for a place to set her one million bags, which included her backpack, a large duffel bag filled with who knows what, and, of course, the bald kitty, housed in his travel case. The case was gray and shaped like a little spaceship, with two long handles like a tote. Veronica's face peeked out of a bubblelike window built into the front of the bag. As usual, he did not seem amused.

"I see you've brought the bat," said Dot.

"Mrrrow," said Veronica, blinking from inside the carrier.

"Is it okay if he comes out?" asked Bree.

Malia winced. "The shredder? Is he going to destroy my entire material life?"

"No! We've made a lot of progress with Dr. Puffin," said Bree. "He's been way less destructive. At our last session, Dr. Puffin said that he's become a peaceful lotus."

"How much do you pay this woman?" asked Dot.

"Veronica is worth it," Bree countered. "His well-being is priceless. And we've cut our sessions back to every other week."

Malia narrowed her eyes. "Fine. Claws can come out. But if he tries anything weird, he's going right back in the cage."

"It's not a cage, it's an ergonomic feline carrying case," corrected Bree, unzipping the top of the vessel in question. Veronica leapt out and started slowly making his way around the room, circling the perimeter and stopping to investigate a bowl of puffed cheese snacks that sat atop Malia's desk.

"Veronica! Those snacks are not part of your journey," Bree said, calmly. Veronica left the snacks alone and moved on to sniffing Malia's pencil cup. "Dr. Puffin taught us that," she added with a shrug.

"Okay. It's time for this Best Babysitters board meeting to come to order!" Malia said, clapping her hands three times for emphasis. "As you know, we have a lot of things to discuss."

In an attempt to put the lessons from her internship with Ramona Abernathy to good use, Malia had taken it upon herself to rebrand some elements of the Best Babysitters organization. Their regular fees were now referred to as "revenue." Their regular meetings were no longer "club meetings"—they were "board meetings."

"Can it still be a board meeting if there isn't a board?" asked Dot. "I mean, we're the only members of the entire organization. It's not like we have investors or an advisory committee or anything."

"Yes, it can be a board meeting because we are the board.

Meeting." Malia sighed. "Anyway! The first order of business is to talk about whether we even have a business."

"Well, that's depressing," said Bree.

"I think it's time for a rebrand. Dot! You're smart. Bree! You're good at theater. I think we start to market ourselves as a full-service babysitting service. We don't just watch children. We provide tutoring in all subjects! And we also help them participate in the arts! We can make special kid-kits organized by different subjects."

Her friends just blinked at her, skeptically.

"If you have any other ideas, I'd be happy to hear them. In the meantime, our only client is somehow Zelda Hooper."

"That was so weird," said Bree. "I can't believe it even happened."

"Well! It's about to happen again," said Malia. "Because Zelda's mom has requested us for another job."

"What?! Why?" Bree apparently wasn't holding back today.

"I know, it doesn't make sense to me, either." Malia shrugged. "But a job is a job. And it's literally all we have."

"Yes, but we're babysitters, not bully-sitters," said Dot, her red-manicured fingers sweeping her hair back into a ponytail.

"Why would Zelda agree to do that again? It was so awkward and terrible," said Bree.

"I get the sense that Zelda isn't agreeing to much of anything," said Dot.

"Look, we are going to get our business back from the au pairs . . . eventually. But until we do, we don't have another source of income right now. So as weird as this whole Zelda thing is, I think we should just move forward with it." Malia had taken to saying things like "move forward" and "circle back" and "table this for another day," which was all Ramona's influence. Half the time her friends had no idea what she was talking about—half the time, Malia didn't even know what she was talking about—but it made her feel very official.

"Everyone!" Bree said. "I have a *very* important announcement." She paused for effect.

"I hope it's a brilliant idea about how to get our business back," said Malia.

Bree unzipped her giant duffel bag and pulled out a rolled-up poster board. Malia breathed in, preparing herself for whatever was next. When Bree made a poster, she really meant business.

"I swear, if this is about Veronica, the cat OR the pop star—" Dot whispered to Malia.

Bree carefully unfurled the poster. Malia expected it to be

covered with pictures of kittens, or cats, or celebrities holding cats. Or maybe dollars bills, and ideas for ways to earn them.

Instead, it was covered with pictures of lizards.

"I am pleased to introduce . . . the salamander," Bree said.

"We already know the salamander," Malia said. "We just encountered it the other day. Are you trying to upset me? I haven't stopped thinking about how we might have squished a bunch of them."

"Yes, but how much do you know about the salamander's migratory patterns?" Bree pressed on.

"Salamanders make an annual migration during their mating season, when they leave hibernation and head to bodies of water to breed," Dot replied.

As she often did, Malia wondered where Dot got all her useless knowledge.

"And are you aware that this is happening right now?" Bree pressed on. "Right here in Playa del Mar?"

"No, I was not aware of this," said Malia.

"WELL, IT IS! And it's very dangerous!" Bree's voice grew higher and more impassioned with every word. "According to a number of studies I've read, salamanders are currently migrating by the hundreds—maybe even the thousands!—and their path takes them right across Waveland Avenue. That's why we nearly killed them. And it's not just us—they're getting squished by cars and bikes and vans and trucks and scooters." Bree looked horrified.

And of course, it was horrifying, Malia thought. No creature should get squished by random vehicles just for trying to live its life.

"Something must be done!" said Bree.

"I agree! But what can we do?" asked Malia.

"Well, I'm still in the process of trying to figure that out," said Bree. "But I think, for starters, it would be good to recruit volunteer crossing guards to make sure the salamanders can migrate safely."

"Salamanders?" Chelsea, Malia's evil older sister, appeared in the hallway outside Malia's bedroom door.

"How is it that you can get a perfect SAT score but you can't figure out how to knock?" Malia grumbled.

"I thought I heard something about salamanders," Chelsea said, ignoring Malia's tone.

"Yes, a salamander. It's a thing that's slimy like you," said Malia, kicking the door shut with one foot. Even through the closed door, she could hear Chelsea's loud *humph* and her footsteps retreating down the hallway.

"Anyway," said Malia.

"Anyway," Bree continued, "I'm bringing this up today because the salamanders need our help. We have to figure out a way to save them. You're my best friends, and I'd never be able to do this without you."

"You got it," said Malia. She felt her eyes growing wide as ideas began dancing in her brain. "You know, this could also be a really great way to get the word out there about Best Babysitters. We could tell everyone that we're donating a third of our proceeds to a good cause."

"Maybe we could even plan some sort of salamander awareness rally, hosted by Best Babysitters!" Bree said.

"Yes!" Malia loved this idea. "And when the parents see what good work we're doing for the community, they won't be able to resist wanting their kids to spend time with us!"

"I'm on board. And I'll do whatever it takes," said Dot. She stopped to reconsider. "As long as it doesn't involve any costumes, or singing. Or public declarations in favor of Veronica — the person, not the cat." These were valid points, as with Bree, you could never be sure.

"This is even more of a reason to keep our business going!" Malia exclaimed. "The salamanders are depending on us!"

Bree started to cry, just a little. It almost made Malia want to cry, too, but she kept it together.

Malia remained a bit confused about what was expected of her when it came to solving the lizard problem. But it felt nice to care so passionately about something that could also help their business. And she had no doubt that with hard work and a little time, all their issues (both human and salamander) would be solved. If, that is, Zelda didn't squish them all first.

CHAPTER FIVE

Dot

Faced with the possibility of going out of business, Dot accepted a job that even a zookeeper couldn't handle. She had agreed to babysit the three Morris brothers who were so terrible, they made the prospect of being dropped in a swimming pool full of hungry piranhas seem fun. And she had agreed to do it alone. She had no choice, really—Malia was frantically working on ways to drum up new business (including this nightmare of a job), and Bree was hanging flyers for a "Save the Salamanders" rally she was holding at the gazebo tomorrow afternoon. Given the circumstances, Dot knew they had to accept whatever paying jobs they could get. She just hoped she wouldn't have to pay for this one with her soul.

"CAN YOU GET US A PIZZA?" yelled Smith, the moment their mom had disappeared from sight.

"No," said Dot. "It's not time for a meal."

"Our other sitters always get us a pizza," said Chase.

Dot highly doubted this was the case.

"I'm not falling for that," she said. "And I don't care what your other sitters do. I am not them."

"YOU SUCK!!!!!!!!!!!!!!!!!!!!" yelled Smith, at a volume typically reserved for use at stadium events.

She had been here all of four minutes, and Dot already had a headache. She wondered if maybe their other sitters did resort to things like ordering pizza just to make the yelling stop.

"Hey, lady! What's the scariest thing you've ever seen?" asked Chase.

"HAVE YOU EVER SEEN A SHARK?" asked Smith.

"Have you ever seen a tarantula?" asked Clark.

"HAVE YOU EVER SEEN A DEAD BODY?" yelled Smith. Was this child not capable of speaking at a regular volume?

"How about we use our indoor voices?" Dot suggested.

"I AM NOT AFRAID OF DEATH BECAUSE I AM THE LORD OF THE DARKNESS!" Smith screamed.

At this rate, Dot almost believed him.

"Hey! Sitter lady!" yelled Clark.

"My name is Dot."

"Did you just say your name is SNOT?" said Chase.

"No, you know my name is Dot."

"YOUR NAME IS SNOT AND YOU ARE MADE OF PHLEGM AND YOU ARE GOING TO PERISH IN THE DRAGON'S CAVE!" yelled Smith, who was arguably the worst of the three.

"Yes!" Chase chimed in. "The dragon's cave."

"ALL WHO ENTER THE DRAGON'S CAVE WILL BE CURSED!" screamed Smith. And then he legitimately roared, like some kind of ogre or orc or some other creature that Dot didn't read enough fantasy novels to know about.

"All right, how about we take this party outside?" Dot asked. She didn't want to reward the boys for acting like terrors, but she reasoned that some fresh air might do everyone, including her headache, some good.

A minute later, they all clambered out of the house, the boys running like race horses down the front walkway.

"IT IS TIME TO AWAKEN THE SPAWN OF THE DRAGONS!" yelled Smith, tearing down the sidewalk. He started scream-singing an earsplitting song that was seemingly meant to mimic an electric guitar.

"Spawn of the dragons!" echoed Chase, joining in the singing.

The boys sang the nonsense song all the way to the park. It was only seven blocks, but it felt like an eternity. Dot could only hope that the playground, with its assortment of things to climb on, would prove to be a worthy diversion.

But upon arrival at the park, Dot was confronted with a very different reality. Indeed, the playground itself was blissfully unoccupied, and the boys took off running in its direction. But in order to get there, she would need to walk past a very disturbing scene. On the grassy knoll in the center of the park sat the Larsson triplets—Thor, Ruckus, and Bronson—with another babysitter.

They were spread out on a red-and-white-checkered blanket, with a large straw picnic basket and an assortment of food. It looked like something out of *Mary Poppins*. The children sat eating quietly—using real plates and actual cutlery, like they were dining with the queen. It was incredibly civilized—aka, the stark opposite to the bedlam that was Dot's current existence.

The au pair gave a little wave.

"*Bonjour*!" she said.

Dot waved back. *Ugh.* Her headache immediately felt worse.

"Hello," Dot said, in what she hoped sounded like a friendly tone.

"Isn't this a lovely day we're having?" said the girl. Indeed, she had a French accent. And curiously perfect-looking hair.

"Are you Genevieve's sister?" Dot asked.

"Oh! You know Genevieve?" Now the girl's face visibly brightened.

"I mean, I don't *know* know her," Dot clarified. "I've only met her maybe once."

"Dot used to be our babysitter," Ruckus piped up.

"Yeah, until our mom fired her to hire you and your sisters!" Thor offered, ever so helpfully.

"This is Sophie. She speaks French and makes crepes, which are French pancakes," Bronson said.

"Dot only knows how to make American pancakes," Ruckus added, unnecessarily.

Dot wished the ground would spontaneously open and swallow her up. Instead, she continued to stand there, feeling humiliated, hoping the triplets had nothing left to say. Also, what was wrong with her pancakes? They were delicious, with or without syrup (but especially with it).

"Mm." The girl nodded, offering a polite, tight-lipped smile. "Well, I'm sure Dot's pancakes are . . . fine. Anyway, thank you for stopping by! It was so lovely to meet you." She flicked her perfectly tousled hair over her shoulder, showing off her perfectly manicured red nails. Dot wondered if the sisters all shared grooming products.

The three little boys Dot was in charge of watching had already done a number on her self-esteem, and now the three boys she used to watch had made her feel even worse. Dot shuffled away as quickly as possible, hoping this would be the extent of their communication for the day.

Over on the playground, the boys had gathered at a rickety old jungle gym in the shape of a spider. But instead of climbing on top of it, they stood underneath it, where they had made a discovery.

"Whoa!" Clark called.

"Sick," said Chase.

"IT'S A DEAD BODY!" yelled Smith.

Dot's heart froze. She got closer to the commotion to see the boys circled around a dead salamander. The sight of it made her feel sad and even more concerned for the plight of the lizards. And it *definitely* wasn't something the kids should be handling.

"Boys! Stand back. Do not touch it," Dot cautioned. "It could give you, like, leptospirosis!"

"YOU'RE A LEPTOSPIROACH!" yelled Smith, as he scooped up the salamander with both hands and took off running. Clark and Chase laughed and followed right behind him.

"YOU CAN'T TAKE THIS LIZARD FROM ME!"

Dot watched the three of them sprint away, running past the choreographed picnic. She deeply regretted the decision to come to the park, or to ever take up babysitting, for that matter.

"WE MUST SACRIFICE THIS TO THE LORD OF THE DARKNESS!" called Smith, climbing up on a park bench. Which technically didn't make sense, because just earlier, he had referred to himself as the Lord of the Darkness. Unless he was referring to himself in the third person. Either way, this was bad.

"I'm serious! Dead animals carry all sorts of diseases. Put that down!" said Dot.

"Awesome!" said Clark.

"Yeah," Chase agreed. "We should eat it!"

Dot had no choice—it was time to resort to lying. "Do you want your fingers to fall off?" Dot asked. "Tonight?"

The boys stopped in their tracks.

"That happens?" Chase looked frightened.

"Yes," said Dot. "All the time. That's what happens when you handle dead things."

"That's not true, my cousin Craig collects dead bugs," said Clark. "And he touches them all the time."

"Your cousin Craig probably didn't want to scare you with the truth. But lizards are a special case. The ghost of the salamander will come to your house tonight and make your fingers fall off!" Dot said. "Unless you put it down RIGHT NOW."

Smith dropped the salamander.

"IT'S FINE I DIDN'T REALLY WANT TO PLAY WITH THE LIZARD THING ANYWAY!"

"Yeah, because it's time to play guitars!" Clark started scream-singing the electric guitar sound again. All three boys started jamming on imaginary guitars, thrashing their heads and screaming at a volume that was likely disturbing people in the next town over. Smith did a complicated split-jump off the park bench and landed—unharmed, save for a few broken branches—in a nearby bush.

Dot just stood there, horrified.

How was this her reality? She was capable of memorizing entire pages of verse, of solving complex equations, of reciting the periodic table of elements in under a minute flat. She was even capable of calming a screaming baby! But figuring out how to handle these three little boys required a sorcery beyond her current pay grade.

Sophie and the Larssons had packed up their picnic and now strolled—it really was a stroll, Dot thought, so calm and collected—in the direction of where the madness was unfolding.

"*Bonjour, Dot!*" she said, in this impossibly melodic way, like she was Maria from *The Sound of Music*.

"*Bonjour, Dot!*" parroted all three Larsson kids.

Dot tried very hard not to hurl.

"How are things over here?" asked Sophie.

"I'm well!" said Dot, hoping that if she put up a convincing enough front, she might distract everyone from noticing the monsters nearby. "Things are good!"

Sophie seemed skeptical. She leaned in conspiratorially, placing one hand on Dot's shoulder. "If you need any, um, *advice*, you can always ask me," she said, in her annoyingly adorable accent. "It seems like you may be in a little over your head."

Then Sophie looked at Dot the way one would regard

an injured stuffed animal that had been left in the backyard. Overnight. In the rain. It was a look Dot was unaccustomed to receiving, and she didn't like it one bit. Dot wasn't a failure. Historically, she was an excellent babysitter. And she didn't like that anyone would think otherwise.

"Thanks, but I think I've got this under control," she said, just as Smith jumped off the top of the spider jungle gym and landed directly on top of Chase. They collapsed into a tangled pile of boy. Chase wailed and immediately burst into tears.

Sophie smirked.

"Okay, then. Good luck, Dot!" she said, with a little wave. Then she and the Larsson triplets walked off into the distance, Sophie swinging the picnic basket and all of them singing a French nursery rhyme that Dot wasn't cultured enough to recognize.

"WHAT IS THAT AWFUL SOUND?" yelled Smith, who was apparently enjoying the French song about as much as Dot. "GO AWAY!" he screamed into the distance. "AND DON'T COME BACK."

For once, Smith had the right idea.

CHAPTER SIX

Bree

It was a beautiful day in Playa del Mar. The sun was shining. A light breeze was blowing. The smell of wildflowers drifted through the air. It was the perfect day for an outdoor gathering at the gazebo at the end of the cul-de-sac.

Bree was hosting the first community meeting of Save the Salamanders, and she had to say, she was both thrilled and impressed with the turnout. It wasn't a very large gazebo, by any means, but it was filled to the brim with concerned citizens. Malia and Dot sat in the front row, offering their support. Next to them sat Veronica, in his cat case, looking remarkably unimpressed.

"Welcome!" Bree said. "And thank you for joining me to fight this most important of fights."

There was a tiny smattering of applause, though it seemed to come mostly from Malia.

"Today we gather to ensure the safety of our neighbors, the salamanders." Bree spoke with authority, the way she had seen people do on TV. "They are a humble but noble species. It is our duty to be their voice. Or their eyes. Or their feet, or something. It is our duty to keep them safe." She was especially proud of that last line.

A hand shot up in the crowd.

"Yes! Do you have a question?"

"Are there going to be snacks?" asked a boy. "The sign said there would be snacks."

"Yes. But patience!" said Bree. "The snacks will come. First, we must discuss the task at hand: saving the salamanders."

"Okay but, like, how long before we get to the snacks?" the boy asked.

Bree sighed. "Do you prefer sweet or savory?"

"What have you got?"

"Cheese puffs, chocolate chip cookies, and pretzels," Bree said. "You know what, why don't you guys just pass these around now?" She handed off a grocery bag to Dot and the snacks started making the rounds. Sometimes dealing with people her own age could be more challenging than wrangling children.

With everyone contentedly chewing, Bree returned to the official agenda.

"Okay, people. As I was saying. There are lizards in peril!" She wasn't afraid of a dramatic spin. This was serious business, and she needed everyone to understand just how much was at stake. She explained the basics, like lizard anatomy and fun facts, and the specifics, like how sweet lizards were being squashed right here in their own hometown.

"Are there any questions?" she asked.

A hand shot up. It was the snack boy again.

"Do you have any lemonade or anything?" he asked.

Bree kind of wanted *him* to get squished in the middle of Waveland Avenue, but she resisted the urge to share that.

"You know, I'm not a convenience store," Bree said. "Lemonade is kind of heavy, and I couldn't carry it here."

Bree was well aware of the pretzel thirst factor. This was why she had planned to wait to share the snacks at the end, when everyone could go find a beverage elsewhere.

"I have drinks!" said a voice. Bree looked around to see where the sound was coming from. A few rows back, there sat

Chelsea Twiggs, also known as Malia's older sister. Also known as the actual devil, if the devil were a seventeen-year-old girl with perfect hair and perfect grades and perfect posture. She stood and floated over to Bree, toting two giant grocery bags as though they weighed nothing at all. "I have pastries, too!" she said, beaming in that Chelsea way of hers. The crowd actually cheered.

Bree looked over to her friends, where Malia was very dramatically rolling her eyes.

With the ease of a seasoned Girl Scout troop leader, which she probably was, Chelsea passed around paper cups, sparkling fruit beverages, and a box full of chocolate-filled pastries. Everyone enthusiastically accepted a snack except Malia, who crossed her arms defiantly.

"What IS this?" Dot asked through a mouthful of pastry.

"*Pain au chocolat*," said Chelsea, matter-of-factly.

"WHERE did it come from?" Dot crammed another enormous piece in her mouth.

"This new bakery in town," she said. "All their stuff is really amazing."

"IT'S SO FLAKY!" Dot exclaimed. "I want to live inside of one forever!"

Bree wished that Dot would feel half this much excitement

for salamander welfare, but was glad that at the very least, she seemed enthusiastic about *something*.

"Okay, now back to the salamanders," Bree said, trying to steer everyone back on track.

"WHERE is the bakery where this came from?" asked a girl with pigtails.

"It's called Jolie Pâtisserie!" said Chelsea, pronouncing the words in what Bree thought was a very unnecessary French accent. "It's in the town center, with a huge red-and-white awning. You should check it out!" She offered Bree a smile. "Now back to the salamanders, shall we?"

"Thank you, Chelsea. As I was saying, it is our job to keep the salamanders safe. Gandhi once said, 'You can judge a nation by how it treats its animals,' and the same is true for a town. What kind of town is Playa del Mar? Are we the kind of town that squashes its salamanders? Or are we the kind of town that stands up and does what is right?"

There was another smattering of applause, and this time it was more than just Malia.

"We are faced with a very important choice: the choice to squish the lizards or to raise them up. Let us make the right decision!"

Presenting her proposal to the group made Bree feel

different than she had ever felt before. When Bree was speaking, she wasn't worried about what anyone might think of her. She wasn't worried about whether she was saying the right thing. She wasn't even worried about the stuff she normally worried about, like her homework and Veronica and whether she could wear a jean jacket with beading or if that would be too similar to glitter and make Veronica go bonkers. When she was speaking, Bree lost track of time and space. She felt like the best version of herself. She felt like she was exactly where she was meant to be.

After the speech, everyone filed out of the gazebo, buzzing with energy. While Dot and Malia went to talk to their school friends Shoko and Mo, Bree stayed behind for a moment to gather up her posters. She hoped she had done enough to inspire the masses to do their part.

"Bree, that was spectacular!"

Bree looked up to see Chelsea standing before her. Chelsea was seventeen, and talking to her felt like talking to a grown-up. That, combined with all the terrible things Malia had told her about Chelsea and all the horrible things Bree had seen for herself over the years, made her feel a little bit nervous.

"So, Bree, I was thinking." Chelsea leaned in conspiratorially. "We should absolutely combine forces."

"Forces?" said Bree.

"To save the salamanders!" Chelsea shifted the weight of her brown leather backpack from one shoulder to the other. "Just picture it. You could bring your tremendous enthusiasm to the project, and keep inspiring everyone to get involved. And I could use my incredible business acumen and talent for networking to spearhead some top-notch grassroots efforts!"

Bree was skeptical. For starters, she didn't understand a bunch of the words Chelsea had just used. If Bree decided to partner with Chelsea, Malia would probably be mad and accuse Bree of siding with the enemy. And, maybe most important, could Chelsea really be trusted?

Still, Bree had to admit that Chelsea would make a very effective partner. She was older and smarter and good at pretty much everything. She knew about stuff like networking and business plans. Plus, she could drive.

"Mayyyyybe," Bree said, very slowly.

"Bree." Chelsea inhaled. "I do not understand your hesitation. Here you are, standing in the gazebo to drum up support from the community, and I am offering my services to you. This is an incredibly worthy cause, and I am very dedicated to it. As you are no doubt aware, I have a very diverse skill set, and I plan on using it to save those salamanders one way or another. We might as well do it together."

Bree tried to come up with some argument, but she couldn't think of a thing. Chelsea *was* making some good points. And her help would be valuable.

"So?" Chelsea batted her eyelashes. "What do you say?"

Bree glanced around, wishing one of her friends (or really, like, anyone) would rush up and tell her what to do. But no one was around. Bree would have to figure this one out for herself.

Chelsea held out her hand, and Bree shook it. As of that moment, they were in business.

CHAPTER SEVEN

MALIA

The only thing sadder than walking to another weird babysitting job at Zelda's house was walking to another weird babysitting job at Zelda's house WHILE discussing how there were no other jobs except the Morris boys because the au pairs had stolen them all. Malia realized she was having another one of those moments that made her appreciate how good she'd had it before.

She'd taken every measure she could to make Best Babysitters seem more relevant. They were now billing themselves as both babysitters and homework helpers, and Malia had sent out an email blast advertising this new service. They had even made kids' culture-kits, featuring coloring pages with famous works of art and flash cards with vocabulary words in four different languages. But at the end of the day, Malia, Bree, and

Dot weren't interesting and well-traveled and multilingual. They were still just three local girls who were self-taught in the ways of caring for children. So, despite their best marketing efforts, no one had really cared.

Too soon, Malia found herself standing on that doormat telling them to *Shut the front door!* She wished she could shut Zelda's front door, forever and ever, and never open it again.

This time Zelda was the one to greet them at the entrance.

"Well, look who it is," she said, as though she'd been excitedly awaiting their arrival.

Malia had expected more of the same, but today, Zelda was talkative from the start. "We should hang out in my room!" she suggested, which was new. They hadn't been allowed in Zelda's room before, and they had no idea what it even looked like.

Malia was surprised to discover that Zelda's room resembled any other thirteen-year-old's room. It had a black-and-white-striped rug and a white lacquered desk and a bookshelf full of books and knickknacks. Striped curtains hung in the two windows. Malia supposed the black bedspread was a little dark. But beyond that, there were no outward signs that Zelda was actually a miserable force of evil.

"Please, have a seat." Zelda gestured grandly to the carpet.

"How was everyone's day?" she asked, like they were old friends. In a way, Malia supposed they were.

Malia flashed back to their younger days at Playa del Playtime, the local preschool next to the Chicken Resort, a fried chicken restaurant whose name made no sense because it was definitely not a resort of any kind, especially for the chickens. Three-year-old Zelda had sported a bowl haircut with thick bangs, and always wore floral dresses and frilly socks. Ten years later, it wasn't just the physical stuff that was unrecognizable. Back then, she had also been nice.

The sweet Zelda of yore had shared her snacks and her secrets, and always held hands with Malia as they walked back and forth from the crafts studio to the playground. She had even given Malia a friendship necklace—a silken cord with a plastic charm in the shape of a yellow dog. Malia still had the necklace in her jewelry box, though of course she hadn't worn it in years.

Their friendship had continued until kindergarten, where they had been excited to discover they were in the same class. Then one spring day, without warning, Zelda marched up to Malia in the middle of the playground and said she didn't want to be friends anymore. Malia could still picture it clearly: standing there, clouds of dust from the sand pit under the jungle gym swirling in the air, not knowing what to say. She hadn't done anything wrong. As far as she knew, nothing had changed. Why didn't Zelda like her anymore?

From that point forward, Zelda morphed into an entirely different person. Gone were the sweet dresses and the frilly socks, replaced with trendy clothes and a perpetually annoyed expression. Zelda didn't roll with a pack, or have a posse, the way the soccer players or the surfers or the drama club did. She was a lone wolf. She preferred to operate alone—Zelda against the world. It was quite the transformation. Sometimes, Malia would think back to that kind little kid and wonder what happened.

"No one wants to tell me how their day was?" Zelda said, reacting to the silence that greeted her.

"My day was fine," said Bree, but offered nothing more. This was an obvious lie, as normally everything with Bree was either wonderful or terrible, but never in between.

"Can I get you anything?" Zelda asked, still playing the perfect hostess. "Water? A snack?"

Everyone shook their heads no.

"Can you believe what happened to Aidan Morrison?" Zelda continued, in a gossipy tone, like a friendly woman at a nail salon. "You heard about it, right?"

Everyone nodded their heads.

Earlier that day, Aidan Morrison's pants had ripped up the back during gym class. Malia—who opted to walk around the perimeter of the soccer field instead of playing basketball—hadn't actually been in the gym when it happened, but it was all anyone could talk about. It was the only time she had ever regretted not participating in a sport.

"It made the craziest noise!" Zelda said. "I've never seen anyone's face turn that color before! He was, like, hot pink." She laughed at Aidan's expense. "So anyway, can I get your opinions on something?"

Zelda was asking for their opinions? Dot and Malia exchanged a confused glance.

"I have to go to my cousin's sweet sixteen next weekend, and I can't figure out what to wear. I was hoping you guys might be able to help me."

Bree visibly perked up at the mention of outfits. "Ooh! Styling clothes is my favorite thing!"

"I know, that's why I wanted to ask you," said Zelda. "And, Dot, you're so chic." Dot seemed to brighten at this, though it was so subtle that Malia couldn't be sure. "And, Malia, your sense of style is so . . ." Zelda paused, trying to find the right word. "Whimsical," she concluded.

Malia was pretty sure that was meant to be a dig, but what more could one expect from Zelda?

"Anyway, take a look at what I have to work with," she continued, opening two big white doors that swung outward to reveal a rather impressive closet. It wasn't quite a walk-in closet, but either side was lined with shelves, and the hanging rack was set back just enough that you could step into the space. It even had an overhead light.

"This is great!" said Bree, dashing into the closet.

"Does this sweet sixteen have a dress code?" asked Dot, slowly slinking across the room.

"Ummm, semi-formal," said Zelda.

"Where is she having it?" asked Malia, stepping into the closet along with Dot. Her classmates had all tried to outshine one another with their extravagant thirteenth birthday parties. The thought of having to go through it all over again when everyone turned sixteen was almost too much for her to handle.

"It's nowhere," said Zelda with an evil grin, "because it doesn't exist."

Then she swiftly closed the doors behind them.

"Wait, what?" Malia turned and tried to push open the doors. They wouldn't budge.

Malia was furious. She couldn't believe they had let this

happen. Of *course* Zelda had had something up her sleeve. They had let their guards down for one minute and now they were trapped in a closet.

"What do you think you're doing?" yelled Bree. "Let us out!"

But Zelda didn't answer. For all they knew, she had left the room.

"Zelda, what the—?" Dot put all her weight behind the doors. But they remained locked.

"This is like one of those escape room shows!" Bree said. "I hate those. They always make me nervous."

"Okay, this isn't as bad as it could be. At least we're not in an elevator. There is no chance of anything crashing." Malia was trying to see the bright side, although it wasn't that bright.

"I'm itchy! Everything itches!" Bree started scratching her arms.

"Just stay calm," Dot instructed.

"WHAT IF THERE ISN'T ENOUGH AIR?" Bree shrieked.

"There is a pretty large gap between the doors and the floor—I think we'll be fine," said Malia.

"Once, when I was four, I got locked in the linen closet,"

Bree said, nearly hyperventilating. "Nobody found me for days."

"Days?" Malia was skeptical. Bree's family could be a little scattered, but days felt like a bit much.

"Okay, not days, but it felt like days. It was definitely, like, a whole day. I got stuck in there after breakfast and nobody found me until just before dinner and I was so hungry and afraid and I still can't be in a room with a towel unless the door is open, at least a little bit."

"Well, luckily there are no towels in here," Dot said. "Just a lot of trendy clothing."

"WHAT IF WE NEVER MAKE IT OUT? WHO WILL TAKE CARE OF MY CAT?" Bree wailed.

"We won't be trapped forever, because Zelda's mom will come home eventually," Malia said.

"Yes," Dot added, "and Zelda will likely let us out before that happens, so she can pretend everything is fine."

No sooner had the words left her mouth than the doors opened.

"Hi, freaks." Zelda was smiling. "Wasn't that fun?"

"Sure, if your definition of 'fun' is torture," said Malia.

"Zelda's definition of 'fun' *is* torture," said Dot.

"Oh! Sweet air!" Bree threw herself onto the ground and began very dramatically kissing the shaggy purple carpet.

Malia's phone vibrated. It was a text from Aidan Morrison. That was weird. She almost never heard from Aidan. He only had her phone number because they had once gotten partnered up on a history project.

Hey Malia. Thanks for getting locked in a closet. Now my pants are only the second most embarrassing thing that happened today.

Malia's heart stopped beating.

"Aidan Morrison knows we got stuck in the closet," said Malia.

"How does he know about that?" Bree looked genuinely confused.

Zelda cackled. "Because I had a camera rigged on the top shelf, and I posted a video clip of you guys stuck in there."

"What?" Dot was furious. "Posted it where?"

"On every single social channel there is."

"Oh my god!" Malia's face went slack. "What if Connor sees it?" Zelda looked intrigued. Malia realized she was admitting her crush and immediately started to backtrack. "I mean, because he's friends with Aidan and Aidan just texted me, so there's a good chance that Connor saw it, too. Along with Bobby and Josh and Henry and all the boys on the soccer team."

"At least you didn't have a total breakdown?" Dot offered.

"Or scratch yourself. Or yell about suffocation," added Bree.

"Look how many views this is getting," said Zelda, delightedly scrolling on her phone.

Suddenly, Malia missed the sound of screaming babies. She missed baby vomit. She missed boogers. She missed the babysitting of actual children, where it was always clear who was in charge.

Malia knew babysitting Zelda would be an annoyance, but before, it was just an annoying secret. Now it had become humiliating as well. With the push of a button (and the slamming of a couple of closet doors) Zelda had taken things to a whole new level.

Already, Malia wasn't looking forward to going to school the next day, where she and her friends would surely be laughed at. This was more than they'd bargained for. Reputations were on the line. Zelda was playing with fire, and Malia hoped she could figure out a way to put a stop to it before everyone got burned.

CHAPTER EIGHT
Dot

Study hall, for most people, was actually a chance to catch up on the homework they still needed to do for the rest of the day. For Dot, it was a chance to catch up on her reading. Since Dot actually enjoyed homework (and, in most cases, found it relatively easy) study hall was the perfect time to read up on what was going on in the world, using her very favorite birthday gift her mom had ever given her: a digital subscription to the *New York Times*.

But today, no matter how much she tried, she found herself reading the same sentence over and over again. Everything she saw reminded her of what was wrong with her life.

Take the current article, for example. It was a story about a woman entrepreneur who was a self-made billionaire. Dot expected it to be inspiring and informative, but instead, the article focused on how much online trolling the poor billionaire was forced to endure. This reminded Dot of Zelda's "locked in the closet" video, which was still making the rounds all throughout the school. Was no one safe? Dot wondered.

Dot's phone pinged with an incoming text message. She was excited to see that it was from Aloysius, boy genius and her all-time favorite babysitting charge. Perhaps he had convinced his mom to fire the French au pairs and was reaching out to share the news.

Are you okay? the text read. **I saw that video about the closet.**

Never mind.

Dot couldn't believe it. The video had apparently made it all the way to the kindergarteners.

"Yes, I'm fine," Dot answered. "Just one regrettable afternoon."

Dot missed Aloysius. His intelligence, his maturity, his empathy. He was such a joy to spend time with. He was the polar opposite of Zelda and those Morris hooligans.

She sighed.

"Heh heh heh," chuckled Aidan Morrison, whose laugh sounded a little like a cross between a goat and a machine gun.

That was the other reason she was having trouble

concentrating on her work. The soccer boys were acting up even more than usual—talking and laughing and occasionally hooting. Though they were sitting all the way across the cafeteria, the sound had a way of intensifying as it traveled through the room.

Dot had no idea what they were laughing at, but she wished they would stop.

"What is going on over there?" she stage whispered to Malia, who was rushing to finish up her environmental science homework.

"Ugh, I don't know, but I'm finding it hard to concentrate on these questions about lichen," she said.

"At least you've gotten to the part about the lichen!" Mo grumbled. "I'm still on the part about the owl pellets."

"Yeah, and I'm about ready to give up," said Shoko, as the boys erupted in a volcano of laughter.

"I mean, WHAT can possibly be so funny?" Mo rolled her eyes.

A moment later, they had their answer.

"WHAT IF WE RUN OUT OF AIR?" Aidan shrieked in a squeaky voice.

"How do closets work?" Ben acted confused.

Josh held up his hand like a door and repeatedly ran his face into it.

They were watching Zelda's video and reenacting the entire thing.

"Oh my god," Malia breathed.

Connor Kelly also sat at the soccer boys' table. Malia stared across the room, her eyes wide. At least he wasn't participating.

Across the cafeteria, Zelda sat alone at a table, taking the whole scene in. She and Dot made eye contact and Zelda winked, snickering to herself.

"By tomorrow, this will be old news," Dot said. She was less than amused by this display, but she had never cared much about what the soccer boys thought of her.

"I am totally humiliated," Malia whined.

Shoko looked up from her homework to offer a look of sympathy. "If it makes you feel better, Zelda has pulled pranks on pretty much everyone before. The only reason people are paying attention to this is because it makes them feel better about whatever has happened to them."

Dot thought those were wise words.

Still, Malia put her head down on the table and sighed into her homework.

Bree, who had been curiously absent from study hall so far, came rushing through the cafeteria doors. As usual, she was carrying a bunch of bags—a backpack, a tote bag, and a large woven rainbow straw bag that looked like it was perhaps meant for the beach. She shuffled up to the table and pulled a bunch of flyers out of the bag in question. The flyers were printed on neon paper the color of a tennis ball and featured a photo of a very friendly looking salamander standing in some grass.

"You guys!" She was out of breath. "I just put Save the Salamander posters on all the community bulletin boards. It has everything anyone needs to know about crossing the street safely and also ways to help."

"That's great!" said Dot. "Do you need our help hanging up the rest of them?"

"No, I was just going to hit all the outside bulletin boards, but there aren't that many. And then Chelsea and I are meeting up to discuss our plans going forward."

Malia picked her head up for the first time since the incident with the soccer boys.

"I'm sorry, what?"

Malia looked to Dot for backup. Dot remained quiet.

"Look, I know you think she's evil—" Bree started.

"No, she *is* evil. I don't see why you have to get involved with her. *We* can help you save the salamanders. Seriously, partnering with Chelsea will be the end of you."

Bree huffed. "No, refusing Chelsea's help will be the end of the salamanders. I'm not becoming her best friend, I'm just working with her on something that we all care about."

Malia's expression remained skeptical.

"She has good ideas," Bree continued, "and good connections. I understand why you're skeptical, but she really wants to help. Plus, there's enough room for ALL of us to save the salamanders. They need all the help they can get."

"Okayyyyy." Malia held up her hands in a sign of surrender. "But don't say I didn't warn you."

Bree looked around the table one more time. "Okay, I gotta go hang the rest of these posters!" she trilled. "See you later!" And with that, she scooted off.

As soon as she was gone, Malia turned to Dot. "I'm telling you, working with Chelsea is going to be the end. Of her, of the salamanders, of everything."

Perhaps she was being a touch dramatic. But when it came to Chelsea, everything was dramatic.

"Speaking of the end," Dot said. "Those three little monsters need a babysitter again, and I am not about to do it alone."

"That's fine. We need to keep them as a client," Malia said.

"So we can all go. We'll all babysit the monsters and we'll all babysit Zelda."

"Zelda?" Dot was honestly surprised. "You're willing to keep the Zelda job even after what just happened with the closet?"

Malia shot her a look of death. "This isn't a matter of preference. We don't have a choice. If Zelda goes away, our business is basically doomed."

She had a point. Still, some things—like dignity—were priceless.

"Maybe we just need a new tactic," Dot tried. "We don't give Zelda a chance to prank us because we don't even engage with her. No speaking, no encouragement, no nothing. We stick together and we stay alert."

Malia nodded solemnly. "That sounds like a plan. And also our only hope."

CHAPTER NINE

Bree

"H**i,** salamander," Bree said, crouching down to get a better look at the little creature.

It blinked and continued on its way, making a slithery run across Waveland Avenue.

"And that's it!" said Bree. "That's all we have to do."

"So we're basically just lizard crossing guards," said Chelsea.

"Yes, but heroic ones. And if we see any traffic of any kind, we flag it down using this sign."

Bree held up a poster she had made, which read *SLOW DOWN! SALAMANDER X-ING!* It didn't glitter, unfortunately, but it was still a marvelous sight to behold. Every letter was a different color.

"Oh!" said Chelsea, with a slight frown. "Well, I suppose there's no way any cars will miss that."

"Then, once the vehicle has slowed, we do whatever we need to to usher any salamanders safely across the street. We might scoot them along, or pick them up and carry them across. You can try to get a sense of their personality and use your best judgment."

"Got it," said Chelsea. "About how many salamanders cross per hour?"

"It varies," Bree said. She actually had no idea.

They sat down on a log. Nothing happened. A frog croaked nearby.

"What's that?" asked Chelsea. There was rustling in a nearby bush. Was it a salamander?

They watched. They waited.

It was a mouse. And it didn't even want to cross the street.

"Ew," said Chelsea.

"So should we use this time to brainstorm our plans?" Bree asked. She had been busy since the rally and was proud of what she had to share. Bree reached into her tote and pulled out a piece of paper folded into the shape of an origami flower. She unfolded it to reveal a handwritten list.

"Great idea!" Chelsea pulled an electronic tablet out of her tote bag. She clicked around to reveal a complicated-looking spreadsheet. "So. I was thinking we should work on defining our mission with a clear, simple statement."

Bree nodded. "That's easy! Save the salamanders."

"Right, sure. But our mission statement should also describe *how* we are going to do that."

"Well, the first step is what we're doing right now: helping them cross the street safely."

Chelsea frowned. "That's not an effective, long-term solution. We can't man this crosswalk twenty-four-seven."

"But we can!" Bree said excitedly. "We just have to raise awareness in the community and then get people to take shifts. Once they see how important it is, I'm sure they'll be happy to volunteer! And then we can have someone here all the time." She rustled through her papers. "I have a bunch of ideas. Like, I was thinking we could do something that involved dressing up like salamanders."

Chelsea looked confused and also a little bit horrified. Bree couldn't understand why. "How will that help?" Chelsea asked.

"Because dressing up like salamanders is festive and a great way to get attention. People will ask *why* we're dressed like salamanders, and then we can tell them about the cause and ask them to sign up for shifts. We could dress up like salamanders to man the crosswalk, or wear our costumes and go door-to-door to try to drum up support. We could even hold a salamander costume contest, where everyone is encouraged to dress up, too!"

Bree loved anything involving costumes. She already knew what she would wear. She could borrow Ariana's sweatshirt with the green cheetah print, which looked a lot like a spotted salamander. She'd pair it with cheetah print leggings and huge round sunglasses that looked like salamander eyes.

"Bree." Chelsea looked at Bree like she had just suggested putting ice cream up her nose. "I think you need to broaden your horizons. Plus, what if you don't get any volunteers?"

Bree hadn't considered that. Wouldn't everyone want to help? "Um, I guess we could hire someone to do it? Like the crossing guards at school. For salamanders."

Chelsea raised an eyebrow. "You want to hire a full-time crossing guard? How will they get paid?"

Bree also hadn't thought about that. "Well, Best Babysitters has offered to put a portion of our proceeds toward the cause." Bree didn't add that they only had two clients right now.

The sound of a vehicle rumbled in the distance.

The girls stood up, clutching the sign in their hands, and took their spot by the side of the road.

"SLOW DOWN!" Bree called. "WATCH THE SALA-MANDERS!"

The car slowed to a stop. The man behind the wheel looked more than a little confused by the two girls holding up a home-made salamander sign.

Bree looked around. Once she confirmed that there was no wildlife underfoot, they stepped aside, allowing the car to pass. It was a little anticlimactic, but it still felt heroic.

As soon as the car was out of sight, Chelsea turned to Bree, all businesslike. "We need to think bigger."

Bree willed her brain to think. "We could have a bake sale or a craft fair."

Chelsea shook her head. "Bree. A bake sale cannot possibly earn the amount of money that we will need to hire someone to be a crossing guard."

"What if it's a really big bake sale? With a prize raffle, too?" Bree's mom's garden club held an annual raffle every summer. Her mom would let Bree choose which canisters to put the tick-ets in, and they never, ever won. Still, the garden club members always seemed happy with however much money they raised.

Chelsea breathed out through her nose. "Bree, you are so lucky to have me. All your little ideas are just so . . . *small*. In terms of the *real* strategic planning for the cause, clearly it makes the most amount of sense for me to take the lead here. You know, to *spearhead the initiative*."

Bree hated Chelsea's "business speak." It was even worse than Malia's. She felt like people only used those kinds of words when they wanted to intimidate people.

Chelsea prattled on. "For example, I bet I could ask Ramona Abernathy to host a special fund-raiser at her home, for prominent citizens of the town. We could call it something like 'A Night for Amphibians.' I can also speak to *What'sUp, Playa del Mar*, you know, the magazine I've been featured in multiple times? I bet they'd agree to run a feature on Save the Salamanders, which should help drum up awareness and support. And those are just a few of my initial ideas. I think we need to take this thing as far and wide as we possibly can."

"Uh-huh," Bree said. She was having trouble keeping up. Chelsea was approaching this cause with the intensity of a speeding car heading straight for a salamander. But Bree tried to remind herself that it was a good thing. She was grateful to have Chelsea's support; she just wasn't exactly sure where she fit into all this.

"I'm a seasoned public speaker," Chelsea continued, "so I can be the official spokesperson. Plus, because I'm older, I come off as more impressive when appealing to important figures." Chelsea crossed her arms and gave Bree a satisfied smile.

Bree suddenly felt left out of her own campaign. She was the one who had cared about the salamanders in the first place. Chelsea seemed more interested in throwing a fancy event and flaunting her giant résumé than she did about helping the little creatures who were counting on them.

Before Bree had a chance to respond, they heard an engine. It sounded incredibly close.

Bree looked to the road, where a teenage boy on an electric scooter was closing in on the crosswalk. Where had he come from? Bree didn't know what to do.

She waved the sign, but the boy didn't stop.

"LOOK OUT FOR THE SALAMANDERS!" Bree yelled.

Still, the boy showed no sign of stopping. He breezed right through the crosswalk, with no regard for the parade of tiny amphibians making their way across.

Bree shut her eyes, afraid of what she might see when she opened them.

She opened her left eye to discover that there had indeed been a salamander casualty.

A lone tear trickled down Bree's cheek.

"This isn't working," Chelsea said, simply.

Bree wasn't sure if Chelsea was referring to their brainstorming session or their salamander-saving efforts, but either way, she was right. Just hiring a crossing guard wasn't going to be enough. There were currently two of them standing right there, and look what had happened.

"I have another idea," Chelsea continued, and in that moment, Bree was glad. "I can reach out to Bianca Salamanca. She's a wildlife specialist at Playa del Point University, and she's incredibly well-respected. I know her through my work with Ramona Abernathy, and I bet she'd be willing to help us. She could act as a consultant and give us some advice."

That sounded good to Bree. From where she currently stood, it seemed like both she and the salamanders needed all the help in the world.

CHAPTER TEN

MALIA

Only a truly hopeless situation could make them return to Zelda's, but that was the predicament they were in. Their options were to either give up babysitting altogether— or to spend time with the world's biggest bully (or else three little bullies named Smith, Clark, and Chase). And so, once again, they found themselves making the walk down Zelda's street.

"Remember the new plan," said Malia, like a drill sergeant. "We stick together. We do not speak. We do not engage with Zelda. We do not do anything she says, we don't try anything she suggests, and we stay alert, no matter what."

Dot nodded.

Bree gave a little salute.

"And no matter what," Malia commanded, "our job is to stay calm. If we get nervous or afraid, we run the risk of getting distracted and opening the door for her to do something tricky. The goal is to be cool and collected."

And then it was time.

Bree rang the doorbell and a few moments later, Zelda's mom answered. Today, her red hair was secured on top of her head in a messy topknot. She wore a lime green jumpsuit paired with purple metallic sneakers. It was the kind of outfit that sounded weird in theory, but somehow, on Zelda's mom, it looked good.

"Hello, girls! I'm so glad you're here," she greeted them. "I have a surprise: I'm dropping you girls at Marvelous Ray's!"

Zelda's mom looked at them expectantly and Malia forced herself to give an enthusiastic smile.

"Hooray," cheered Bree. Even the likes of Zelda Hooper was not enough to dampen Bree's love for all things Marvelous Ray's.

"Can we order mozzarella sticks?" Dot asked hopefully.

"No, I don't eat dairy," Zelda said, breezing past them on her way out to the car.

Malia heaved a sigh as she buckled herself in. For as long

as she'd been alive, she'd known one thing to be true. If there was any place on this planet that could make a "meh" situation better, it was Marvelous Ray's Arcade. Yet today, Malia felt nothing. Under ordinary circumstances, the thought of a day at Marvelous Ray's would have made Malia ecstatic. But the mere thought of Zelda Hooper trespassing in Malia's sacred space was enough to quash her joy.

Just when Malia thought she couldn't get any lower, Zelda's mom's blue Toyota pulled into a random parking lot and Malia realized they weren't headed to Marvelous Ray's Arcade after all. They were going miniature golfing at Marvelous Ray's new mini-golf center. Golfing with Zelda was, perhaps, the least marvelous thing she could ever imagine.

Malia had never understood miniature golf. Putting was definitely not fun. It was a lesser version of a sport that was known for its overly civilized clap. On what planet could that ever be appealing? Still, at least Zelda's mom was thinking outside the box.

"This place is supposed to be state-of-the-art!" Zelda's mom trilled. "I was just reading about it in the *Playa del Mar Sunday Star.* Apparently every hole has a unique theme, and some of them are really something!"

Zelda, in typical fashion whenever her mom was present, said nothing.

"I've been wanting to go here since it opened!" said Bree, all hopefulness and sunshine.

"Did you know the origins of golf date all the way back to 1497?" said Dot.

"No, because I've never wanted to know anything about golf," said Malia.

"We're here!" Zelda's mom said, guiding the car into a parking spot. "Have a wonderful time! I'll be back to pick you up in an hour and a half."

As promised, the course was huge. There were windmills and giant sculptures of animals and towering fountains with mer-people. Weirdness stretched as far as the eye could see.

"Whoooooooa," breathed Bree, awestruck.

"Does this change our plan of attack?" Dot asked, selecting a purple putter from a rack of multicolored clubs.

"Not really," said Malia, grabbing a blue putter. "Just keep our engagement to a minimum and avoid being videotaped."

The first hole was badger themed. The object was to get the golf ball into the badger's cave. Upon successfully doing so, an animatronic badger would pop up and sing a creepy song.

Right off the bat, Zelda got a hole in one.

"Lucky shot," Malia muttered. But it took her six incredibly clumsy strokes to finally make the badger sing.

"Jeez. Have you ever played golf before?" asked Zelda.

"Not really," said Malia.

"It was a hypothetical question, because that much was obvious," said Zelda.

Malia must have looked genuinely hurt, because something in Zelda seemed to shift.

"I'm just kidding," Zelda said. "You aren't *that* bad."

They were gathering their balls up in preparation for the next hole when Bree stopped in her tracks.

"CLOWN!" shrieked Bree. It was a long-known fact that there was nothing in the universe Bree enjoyed less than encountering a clown. And this clown—at least twelve feet tall, with clouds of red foam hair that extended in all directions as far as the eye could see—was more than she (or, really, anyone) could handle. From hidden speakers, the clown laughed a sinister laugh, over and over and over again.

The objective was to get the ball to roll into either of the clown's two giant nostrils.

"I don't think I can do this," Bree whispered.

"Sometimes, the only way out is through," said Zelda.

"My mom says that," said Dot, her voice dripping with judgment.

"Just don't look him directly in the eyes," said Malia. This was practical advice as well, since the clown's eyes were two pinwheels, and they were very distracting.

Bree squeezed her eyes shut and swung her club haphazardly in the general direction of the clown. The golf ball flew up into the air, bounced across a neighboring green, splashed through a decorative fountain, and ultimately landed in a sand trap, all the way at the very first hole.

Bree gingerly opened her eyes. "Did I win?" she asked.

"No. I actually think you might be disqualified," said Dot.

Bree frowned.

Then, from somewhere behind the menacing clown face, Malia heard a laugh. It was not the automated menacing clown laugh, though that was still happening. It was THE laugh. The laugh that haunted her dreams.

Malia tiptoed over to a nearby walrus statue and peered around its tusk.

Sure enough, at the third hole—indeed, the hole *right in front of them*—three boys were trying to putt into some sort of igloo. And one of the boys was HIM.

Malia immediately took back every negative thing she had ever thought about golf or Zelda's mom or Marvelous Ray's marvelous business plan. This was, without a doubt, the most wonderful day.

"Maybe Bree's right. This clown is kind of creepy. Let's speed up so we can move on to the next hole," Malia urged the rest of the group. The faster they moved, the sooner Bree would no longer have to look at the clown, and the faster Malia would get to look at Connor. It was a win-win.

"What's the matter, are you trying to speed things up to distract from what a horrible golfer you are?" teased Zelda.

"Quite the opposite," Malia shot back. "I'm trying to lessen the time you spend suffering."

"Well, then. How about we let the score card settle that?" Zelda said, as she made the perfect putt. The ball sailed beautifully down the AstroTurf green, landing right inside the clown's left nostril. It was a big win for Zelda, but no matter. Malia would settle for whatever would move them on to the next hole as soon as humanly possible.

The girls rounded the walrus and arrived at the third hole, which was Antarctica themed. There was a glacier, and a seal, and a penguin . . . and Connor Kelly, who was just teeing up.

Maybe Malia was imagining it, but she was pretty sure that when he saw them, he smiled.

"Hey, Malia!" said Aidan Morrison, catching sight of the girls.

"Move it along, boys!" said Zelda. "There are real players entering the green."

"Are you, like, any good?" said Aidan. "Because Josh has already lost his ball twice."

"Shut up!" said Josh. "I was trying to swing the putter like an actual golf club. Because it seemed more fun."

Malia wondered, as she often did, what was wrong with boys.

"Hey! We should play boys versus girls!" said Zelda, shooting a sly look at Malia.

Wait, what? This wasn't part of the plan. Malia wanted to throw up. She wanted to watch Connor play mini golf, but she didn't necessarily want him to see *her* playing. Especially if she kept playing the way she had been.

"Okay!" said Connor.

"Let's see what you've got!" said Aidan.

Anxiety, Malia thought, her palms sweating. *I've got anxiety.*

Everyone teed up next to a towering statue of a friendly

manatee. Malia wasn't sure what a manatee (a warm-water animal) was doing hanging out on the Antarctica-themed section of the course, but she was willing to forgive it.

Connor was up first. Malia watched as he situated himself just so before hitting the ball—his feet shoulder width apart, his floppy hair flapping ever so slightly in the breeze. The thrill of beholding him quickly gave way to terror when Malia wondered what she looked like while doing the exact same things. He hit the ball—so regal! It rolled gorgeously forward. Malia liked him so much she almost—*almost*—wished that he would win. But not quite. And lucky for her team, Connor's ball got caught in a "glacier" that was actually just a sand trap with a concrete penguin inside.

Zelda was next up. "All right, male identifiers. Watch how it's done."

She teed up and sent the ball careening down the green. Once again, she got a hole in one.

"YES!" Malia screamed, with genuine excitement. Before she even realized what she was doing, she ran up to Zelda and gave her a hug. Shockingly, she did not self-destruct. Even more shockingly, the two girls jumped up and down and Zelda hugged her back.

Then it was Malia's turn.

Malia wanted to keep the bar low. She didn't need to get a hole in one. She didn't even need to get a hole in five. For now, she had very simple goals: to actually hit the ball, and not to throw up. Anything beyond that would be a bonus.

She held her breath and hit the ball. It veered to the left and bounced off the guard rail, which was meant to resemble blocks of ice. "That was so close!" said Bree encouragingly, even though it really wasn't. Not the best shot, but certainly not the worst. Malia would take it.

On the next hole, with a dragon-in-a-castle theme, she even got a hole in two (while Connor's ball rolled sadly into the moat).

At last, they arrived at the final destination: the eighteenth hole. Here, the objective was to get the balls to roll onto a ramp, which would deposit them into a giant purple toilet. After landing in the toilet, they would be swept away forever (unless you paid for another round).

"Weird," said Aidan.

"Yeah," Connor agreed.

"I've never seen a toilet that color before!" said Bree. She seemed excited about this.

Staring at the giant toilet, Malia couldn't help but wonder if this course had been designed by some of the more challenging children they'd babysat for.

One by one, everyone made their putts. Aidan's ball headed straight for the ramp, while Connor's missed completely. Malia realized just how much she really, really liked him, because he was a truly terrible golfer and yet she found all his putts to be masterful.

The two teams were neck and neck. Malia was the last to go, and it all came down to her putt. She needed to get the ball in the hole in three strokes or less if her team was to win.

"Are you ready?" whispered Zelda.

Malia wasn't sure she would ever be ready, but she nodded her head yes.

This was the moment of truth.

Malia stepped up to the ball. She readied her stance and took a deep breath. She said a little prayer, to the effect of *Please oh please oh please oh please let this ball go into the toilet*. And then she let go of control, so to speak, and made her putt.

The ball sailed down the green, headed straight for the purple toilet. As if guided by divine force, it rolled down the ramp and plopped into the toilet water with a satisfying *ker-plunk*. It was a hole in one.

Bree screamed and started jumping up and down. Dot also

seemed excited, though in a more reserved way. Zelda grabbed Malia's hands and started swinging her round and round in a dizzy victory dance.

Malia couldn't believe it. She had never excelled at anything relatively sporty in her entire life. How was it possible that Connor had been there to witness the only moment in which she had ever seemed remotely capable of guiding a ball? She looked toward Connor, who, though he looked decidedly casual about it, had definitely been watching. They locked eyes for a moment, until Connor looked away, running his fingers through his swoopy bangs.

"THIS IS SO EXCITING!" yelled Zelda, still dancing away. "We won! We won!"

This day was turning out to be most unexpected. The first major surprise was that Malia had actually enjoyed some version of golfing. The second was that she could, apparently, be okay at it. But the biggest surprise of all was the discovery that she could kind of sort of enjoy being in the presence of Zelda.

CHAPTER ELEVEN
Dot

"**Y**ARGABLARGABARGA!!!!**"** yelled Smith as he jumped off the back of the couch, landing in an all-too-expert looking ninja crouch.

"Wow, this is already horrible," said Malia matter-of-factly.

"I can see why you needed us here," Bree agreed.

Dot had requested backup for her latest job watching Clark, Chase, and Smith. She hoped three sitters would be enough to handle three rambunctious hyena-children, especially after their surprising success with Zelda the day before. So far, though, they had only been in the boys' company for approximately three minutes and already everyone was at their wit's end.

"Let's play bonkers!" Clark suggested, jumping up and down in the middle of the living room.

"How does that go?" asked Malia.

Dot knew better than to ask such questions.

"BONK!" yelled Smith, picking up a throw pillow and bonking Malia over the head with it. "BONK! BONK! BONK!"

Clark and Chase rolled on the floor with laughter.

Malia froze, seemingly unsure what had just happened.

"I told you," Dot whispered. "They're terrible."

Smith dropped the pillow and started rolling on the ground with his brothers.

"YOU GUYS, I ATE A CUPCAKE EARLIER AND THE ICING WAS THE COLOR OF A SHRIMP! BUT IT DIDN'T TASTE LIKE A SHRIMP BECAUSE IT TASTED LIKE A CUPCAKE!"

All three boys laughed at this, though it didn't seem particularly funny.

"Why does that one always yell?" asked Malia.

"It's an enduring mystery," said Dot.

Bree clapped her hands, getting the boys' attention. "I have an idea! How about you guys get some art supplies and we can all draw together?"

This was sweet. It was also, quite possibly, the most hopefully optimistic thing Dot had witnessed in some time. These boys wanted to set everything on fire. The thought of them quietly coloring was hilarious.

But to Dot's surprise, they seemed to think this was a great idea.

"MARKERS!" yelled Smith, as they sprinted out of the living room, apparently off to gather up drawing supplies like civilized five-year-olds.

"I can't believe they went for that," said Dot.

"Emma and Bailey love to draw," said Bree with a shrug. "Whenever I have to watch them, my secret plan is always to offer them plenty of markers and things to color."

About a minute later, the boys came rumbling back into the living room.

"Look what I have!" Clark thundered, brandishing a piece of paper. Smith and Chase were close behind.

"What's that?" asked Dot. But the minute she saw it, it was clear: It was a badly drawn picture of a giant tombstone in the middle of a cemetery. Across the tomb, scrawled in crayon, was a name: *DOT.*

"I drew a picture of your grave!" said Clark, brightly.

"I can see that," said Dot.

"And I drew a picture of your dead body!" said Chase, waving his own piece of paper in the air. This one featured a horizontal stick figure with two X's for eyes and its tongue sticking out.

"I see. Well, isn't that delightfully morbid," she said.

More than ever, this whole episode made her long for the days of babysitting Aloysius, when the only pieces of paper a child ever handed her were covered in complex equations.

"I DREW A PICTURE OF THE GRIM REAPER!" added Smith. He had actually drawn an unrecognizable blob, but Dot was willing to take his word for it.

"Any other great ideas, Bree?" Dot asked.

Bree looked stricken.

"HEY, NEW SITTER!" Smith yelled, standing inches from Bree's face. "I AM A WOLF! AND I WILL USE MY CLAWS TO TEAR YOU TO PIECES!" Then he howled.

Bree burst into tears.

Satisfied, Smith cackled and started running laps around the coffee table.

"Can we go home now?" Bree sniffed.

"No, because this is our life now," said Dot.

"Remember, he's not actually a wolf—he's a little boy," said Malia, petting Bree's hair. "And he's only five."

"I know," whispered Bree through sniffles. "But why does he have so much rage inside?"

"It seems like they feed off one another's energy, so I think we should divide and conquer. Everyone grab one kid and make sure they don't kill themselves, one another, or anything else," said Malia.

"I don't want the yelling one," said Bree.

"That's fine. I'll take the yelling one," said Malia. "Which one is that, again?"

"That's Smith," said Dot.

"Which one has the toy nunchucks hanging out of his back pocket?" asked Bree.

"That's Chase," said Dot. "You take that one. He's kind of the follower of the group, so he should be the easiest to manage."

That left Dot with Clark, who was currently unaccounted for. After some searching, she found him locked in the upstairs bathroom, drawing more gravestones on the mirror with permanent marker.

"All right, there's been property damage," Dot announced, as she dragged him back to the living room. "It is time to vacate the premises."

The boys acted equally berserk in any setting, but at least outside—in the presence of actual wild animals—there was more space in which to deal with them. Dot just hoped that having three sitters on hand would prevent a repeat of what had happened the last time they went to the park.

"Yes! Park!" said Chase.

"Can we make a fire when we get there?" asked Clark.

"YES! WE WILL LIGHT THE FLAMES OF RE-DEMPTION!" yelled Smith, putting one fist in the air.

Where on earth did they get this stuff?

"No, there will be no fire," said Dot.

"THAT'S WHAT YOU THINK!" he replied, taking off for the front door.

"They don't actually know how to make a fire, do they?" Malia looked worried.

"At this point, I wouldn't put anything past them," said Dot.

A little way down the block, a tree had recently been taken down, its branches neatly arranged in a pile near the curb.

"Look! Swords!" called Chase, pointing excitedly. The boys ran over to the pile, each grabbing a huge branch and brandishing them in the air.

"Um, is that a good idea?" asked Bree.

"SWORDS!" yelled Smith in response.

The boys bashed one another as they walked.

"Be careful!" Malia called.

"NO!" screamed Smith, turning to point his stick at her.

"Yes. We don't want anyone to lose an eye," said Dot.

"THEN I'D BE LIKE CYCLOPS!" called Smith. "AND I COULD MAKE STUFF EXPLODE USING JUST MY EYE!" He made laser beam sound effects.

"I don't think it works that way," said Dot.

"You don't know anything!" Clark roared.

"Yeah! Cyclops is awesome!" Chase added.

"I don't think your parents would be quite as amused," said Malia.

Smith batted Chase in the head with his tree branch. Luckily, Chase didn't appear to be injured, but he was angry and embarrassed. Then he started to cry.

"That's enough!" Malia yelled. "Everyone, sticks down!"

"ONLY POOP CRIES!" yelled Smith. It didn't really make any sense, but it succeeded in making Chase cry harder.

"Actually, crying is a sign of bravery," said Dot, crouching down to Chase's level. "It's brave to express how you feel."

"Nuh-uh, that's dumb," said Clark.

"YOU'RE DUMB!" yelled Smith, sprinting through the park's front gates.

Dot scanned the landscape, where she saw that once again, the au pair brigade had descended upon the park. This time, all three sisters were present, singing melodic songs and calmly offering instructions to their charges. Genevieve and Sophie were nearly identical, except Sophie had bangs perfectly disheveled to match the rest of her hair.

Seemingly all of the neighborhood children were present—the Larssons, the Gregorys, the Woos. They spoke in hushed tones, thoughtfully regarding one another as they moved slowly about the park. It looked like some sort of etiquette convention.

Even Aloysius—Dot's all-time favorite client—was part of the French invasion. He sat alone on a park bench, his small feet swinging beneath him as they did not yet touch the ground. He was engrossed in a giant volume, which looked like the sort of old, classic book that only exists in movies set in the nineteenth century.

"Dot!" he said, with genuine excitement.

Perhaps he had traded up for a fashionable French sitter, but at least he was still excited to greet her.

"What are you reading?" Dot asked.

"*À la recherche du temps perdu*," he said, without missing a beat. "The original version. By Marcel Proust."

Naturally, thought Dot. *What else would a five-year-old genius be reading besides classic French literature?*

"That's lovely," she said, "and very impressive. Are you still focusing on science?" She knew he could be a voracious reader, and he had clearly embraced French mania, but she hoped he wasn't letting go of his natural talent for all things scientific.

"Certainly." He blinked his long, dark eyelashes. "I'm just going through a bit of a French phase right now."

You and everyone else in this town, thought Dot.

Before she could reply, she heard a horrible commotion erupt somewhere behind her. She didn't have to turn around to know who had caused it. Still, nothing could have prepared her for what she saw: The boys had somehow started an actual fire inside a public trash can. Luckily, the fire was contained within the metal cylinder. But unluckily, the flames were growing ever higher.

"This is NOT a barbecue!" yelled Malia, rushing over to the scene.

"I don't know how to put out a fire! How do you put out a fire?" Bree called, manically typing into her phone.

Luckily, Dot had sat through enough science lab safety videos to know what to do. She sprinted over to the sandbox, grabbed an abandoned plastic pail, and filled it with sand. Then she sprinted back to the fire and threw the sand on top. It didn't completely put the fire out, but it dampened the flames.

Dot repeated the whole thing again, and on the second round, the fire sputtered out.

"Noooooooooo!" said Clark.

"VILE SITTER LADY!" Smith hollered, shaking his fists and stamping his feet. He was having a complete meltdown, sort of like at the end of "Rumpelstiltskin" before the imp tears himself in two. "YOU HAVE EXTINGUISHED THE FLAMES OF REDEMPTION!"

"You will pay for this in your next life," grumbled Chase.

Dot felt like she was already paying for it in her current life. In addition to being a babysitter, Dot was now required to be a firefighter. She missed the days when "babysitting" meant simply looking after children, not saving the world from burning to the ground.

CHAPTER TWELVE

Bree

So, have you met her before?" Bree asked, as she and Chelsea walked across the campus of Playa del Point University for their meeting with Bianca Salamanca. Bree was excited to meet a real live wildlife expert, but also a little afraid. A wildlife expert was even more impressive than Veronica's cat therapist, Dr. Puffin. Bree hoped she would manage to say the right things.

"I saw her speak at a benefit once," Chelsea said. "But this will be our first actual meeting."

"What's she like?"

Chelsea looked thoughtful for a moment. "She reminds me a little bit of a lion. But, like, a human lion."

Bree wasn't sure what this meant.

Bianca's office was housed in an old building in a far corner of the campus. It looked like the kind of place where a wildlife specialist would work: The outside of the building was covered with vines, and the inside was full of rooms that were seemingly packed with treasures. The entire building smelled like a combination of dust and takeout.

The moment Bianca opened the door to her office, the human-lion reference became clear. With her voluminous mane of strawberry-blond hair and her commanding presence, Bianca Salamanca was something to behold.

"WELCOME!" Bianca practically roared her greeting. She ushered the girls inside, then bounded across the tiny office, taking a seat in a huge leather chair behind a huge wooden desk. Everything in the office—including the floor-to-ceiling bookshelves—was much too big for the tiny office. Bree wondered how they had managed to fit it all inside. The one free wall was packed with a very full gallery of framed photos of Bianca with every species one could imagine.

"Would you like some water?" Bianca asked.

"Oh, no thank you," Chelsea said, while Bree silently shook her head.

Bianca looked like she was dressed for a safari. Her vest had many, many pockets. More pockets than Bree had ever seen on a single piece of clothing. Her shorts were longer than even basketball shorts, and she wore them with white socks rolled halfway up her calves. Her boots looked like they were designed for climbing mountains or tromping through swamps, and seemed rather out of place in the bookish academic building. Topping it all off was a serious-looking khaki safari hat, worn indoors.

"So, Chelsea, I've been thinking about this predicament ever since you gave me a bit of the backstory on the phone." Bianca stroked her chin as she spoke, once again reminding Bree of a lion. "And I think I've come up with the solution."

Bree was ecstatic. They had been here all of two minutes and already Bianca had solved all their problems!

"The answer is a bridge!"

The girls blinked back at her.

"A bridge!" she repeated, for emphasis. She was so excited by the idea that she hit her fists down on the desk, causing a tiny sculpture of an ostrich to wobble to and fro.

"A bridge?" Chelsea looked skeptical. "Like, a *bridge* bridge? That's a major undertaking. Didn't the Golden Gate Bridge take, like, years to build?"

"Not like a *bridge* bridge. A lizard bridge," said Bianca, like this was a perfectly normal thing to suggest.

"Oh," said Bree. Because, really, what else was there to say?

"Here, have a look-see." Bianca pulled out her phone to provide some visuals.

Bree noticed the phone's background photo was a picture of Bianca hugging a very large lion. Bianca tap-tap-tapped on her phone as she spoke. "It would be a perfectly sound, built-to-scale structure that would allow the lizards to keep the same migratory path, just in an elevated way."

"Has this been done before?" Chelsea seemed skeptical.

Bree was thankful Chelsea was there to ask the right questions.

"Yes! Well, no. Not exactly. At least, not in a suburban environment. But there is no reason why it shouldn't work."

Bianca held up a picture of a grass-covered bridge spanning a highway. It actually looked really lovely, Bree thought, sort of like a park in the sky.

"This here is an animal bridge," Bianca said. "They're becoming more and more common as a way for animals to safely cross human-made barriers like roads and highways."

"Um, that looks like the cost would be exorbitant," said Chelsea.

Even Bree, who had no concept of how much anything except clothing cost, thought it looked pretty expensive.

"Oh, it is! But this one was built for deer, you see," Bianca said. "A salamander bridge would be much, much smaller and thus more affordable. I'll put you in touch with my colleague, who is an eco-architect, and he can take it from here."

"That sounds great!" Bree said, even though it sounded a little intimidating.

Bianca stood, rather abruptly, signaling the end of the meeting. "I have a lecture in twenty minutes, so I'll have to be running. But it was a pleasure to meet you both." She paused. "I cannot possibly impress upon you how very good and important this work is. No matter what happens, you must stay the course. The salamanders are depending on you."

"Thank you, Bianca, this has been most helpful," said Chelsea.

The girls exited the tiny office as Bianca marched down the hallway, off to her next adventure.

The girls made their way out of the building, infused with a new, excited energy. Bree felt like the hero in a movie before any of the action had taken place. She knew she had to save something, and she knew what needed to be done, but she still wasn't sure how it would all go down.

"So I guess we have a plan, then," said Bree.

"Oh, Bree, our plan is just beginning to take shape!" Chelsea waved one hand over her head in an arc, like a leprechaun summoning a rainbow. "Now the real work begins! We'll recruit community organizers and start a grassroots effort to pay for the bridge. We should think big. Maybe we can have a benefit! A gala, even!"

Bree didn't know what a gala was, but she nodded anyway. "So you think we'll really be able to do this?"

Chelsea nodded excitedly. "Absolutely. We just have to think big. I have so many ideas!"

Bree was getting excited, too. Since they'd started working together, Bree had wondered many times if working with Chelsea was a mistake. She could be obnoxious, sure, and she was definitely bossy. She dismissed everyone's ideas and thought she knew everything and had a tendency to talk over everyone in a tone that suggested that whatever anyone had to say wasn't nearly as important. And yes, all those were pretty negative qualities. But her heart was in the right place. She was dedicated to the salamanders and she was a hard worker.

Now Bree was grateful to have Chelsea on board. Because of her, they'd met with Bianca and they had a plan, a real one. And together, they were going to make this bridge happen. They were going to save the salamanders!

CHAPTER THIRTEEN

MALIA

Ladies! Welcome!" Zelda opened the front door, smiling widely like a character on a soap opera. "So good to see you again!" Any traces of angst-ridden Zelda had disappeared, replaced by this happy, overly charming individual. It was a little unnerving.

Malia hadn't been sure what to make of the situation since the day at Marvelous Ray's mini golf. She found it hard to believe that after years of putting up with Zelda's antics, her old friend was apparently back.

"Can I get you anything? A snack? Something to drink?"

"Uh . . . I guess some water would be good," said Bree.

"Would you like tap or sparkling? I have seltzer flavored with essences of cucumber, strawberry, or lemon-lime."

"Strawberry?" said Bree uncertainly, like maybe it was laced with poison.

"How about we all start with the strawberry!" Zelda smiled. "It really is *so* refreshing."

Zelda handed everyone a can of sparkling water, decorated with a picture of a strawberry on a skateboard. "Let's all take a seat at the table, shall we?" She pulled out a chair.

This was bizarre.

Malia gingerly held her chilled can and did as she was instructed.

"How have your days been?" Zelda addressed the group.

"Uh, you know, it's been a day," said Malia.

"Yeah, mine, too," said Zelda, nodding awkwardly. Something was definitely up. She was acting almost like a regular person—a person capable of having feelings. She seemed nervous, and maybe even a little shy.

"Is everything okay?" Malia ventured.

"Yeah! Yes. Everything is great," Zelda said. "I actually, um, had fun with you guys the other day at mini golf."

"Me too!" said Bree.

"It was relatively enjoyable," Dot admitted.

Finally, Zelda took a deep breath. "So. I've been doing a lot of thinking lately. And I feel terrible for some of the things

I've done." Malia blinked, not sure where this little speech was headed. "Like that time I hid an old fish in your locker and it stunk for weeks and weeks. Or the time I started that rumor that you pooped in the art room supply closet."

"That was you?!" Malia had always suspected, but hadn't known for sure.

"The point is, I feel horrible for being mean to you. You've never been anything but kind to me. Remember how close we used to be at Playa del Playtime?" Of course Malia remembered, but she didn't know that Zelda did. "I think we could still be friends, and I'd really, really like to. That is, if you could ever find it in your heart to forgive me."

"Uhh . . . I mean, sure," said Malia. She wasn't sure where Zelda's words were coming from, or if she could believe them. But Malia had to admit she had enjoyed playing mini golf and spending more time with Zelda. Was it possible that some glimmer of her old childhood friend was still in there?

"That's really nice, Zelda," said Bree.

"Why the change of heart?" said Dot.

"I realized that everything is easier when you're nice," Zelda said. "It's fun to spend time with friends, and it feels good to make people happy. I guess I just have a new outlook on life."

Malia couldn't believe what she was hearing, but she was very happy to hear it.

"You know, I had my doubts about you. But I have to admit, it's been really nice spending time with you, too." Malia thought back to the joy they had shared on the eighteenth hole, and the joy they had shared back in preschool. "I hope we can have more good times together."

"Me too," said Zelda. "Speaking of which! I have an idea. Follow me."

She led the girls up the stairs and down a long hallway lined with bookshelves. At the end of the hall, they entered a bright bedroom, with all-white furniture and a skylight overhead. It felt very glamorous and very pristine. Zelda opened a white door and the group stepped into the most ridiculous arrangement Malia had ever seen. From the contents, she gathered it was a walk-in closet, but it was unlike any closet she had ever seen. This was Zelda's mother's fabled fashion headquarters, the place where all her amazing outfits lived, and where they had been strictly forbidden from playing dress-up as little kids. It was big enough to be considered a room. In fact, it was so large, and its contents were so amazing, that if Zelda decided to lock them in *this* closet, they could happily remain in it forever.

One entire wall was lined with white built-in shelves, which were filled with shoes. The shoes seemed to be arranged by type (boots, heels, flats, sneakers) and then by the colors of the rainbow. Another wall was lined with similar shelves, this time filled with handbags. There were rows and rows of clothes on hangers, with every color, pattern, and material represented. In the center, there was an island, with multiple drawers filled with even more magical items. Malia couldn't decide if it was more like a museum or the best store she had ever seen. She didn't even care that much about fashion, but this was impressive, by any measure.

"Whoa," said Bree, breathing heavily.

"What is this?" said Dot.

"My mom's closet," said Zelda. "She lets me hang out in here whenever I want."

"How do you get anything done?" asked Bree, petting a pair of purple velvet boots that looked like they would never match anything. "I would spend all my time in here and never, ever leave."

"You're welcome to try on whatever you want!" Zelda said. "My mom doesn't mind!"

"Reeeeeeeally?" said Bree, who was already in the process of removing a periwinkle faux-fur jacket from its hanger.

"Also!" Zelda opened the top drawer. "This is the sunglasses drawer." She opened another. "This is where the makeup lives." She motioned to the remaining three drawers, near the bottom. "And these are the jewelry. You guys can wear or use whatever you want!"

"Oh my goodness!" Bree, now dressed in the faux-fur jacket and a huge black hat, with an electric yellow structured purse dangling off her arm, made a beeline for the makeup drawer.

"Are you sure your mom really won't mind?" Dot asked, petting a leather bag with sequin lions dancing across it. "I mean, I recognize a few of these things as extremely limited edition."

"How on earth do you know that?" Malia asked. She knew for a fact that Dot was very anti–fashion magazine.

"From the *New York Times*," said Dot. "I have a digital subscription."

"My mom definitely doesn't mind!" said Zelda. "Now that I'm older, I do this all the time. She would be so happy that we're enjoying her stuff."

"Amazing!" said Bree, standing on her tiptoes to peer into a magnifying mirror perched on top of the center island. She smeared a bright pink lipstick all over her mouth, then pressed her lips together to set it.

Malia removed a pair of silver glitter ankle boots from a shelf, excited to try them on. Where did Zelda's mom wear half these things? Malia's mom basically lived in her practical canvas slip-ons. Malia wondered if Zelda's mom had a secret, glamorous life.

"Oh, I left my drink downstairs. I'll be right back!" Zelda made a beeline for the doorway, while the girls continued to ransack the shelves.

"This is better than visiting the mall!" said Bree.

"Seriously," said Dot, spinning in a floor-length silk trench coat. "It's more like visiting a museum."

A moment later, Zelda appeared in the closet doorway—but she was not alone. She was with her mother.

How was Zelda's mom back already?

"Your closet is amazing!" said Bree, who was now wearing at least thirty percent of the items from the jewelry drawer.

Zelda's mom stood, silently taking in the scene—the many items no longer in their regular locations, the makeup smeared across the girls' faces. Her expression—like the villain in a horror movie just before they snap—made it immediately clear that spending time in the enormous closet was *not* okay with her after all. All traces of the sweet woman were gone. Zelda, too, was wearing the evil smirk she had become known for. Now Zelda and her mom looked even more like twins.

"What the—" Zelda's mom breathed. She could barely choke the words out.

Zelda—a very strange, unrecognizable version of Zelda —burst into tears.

"This is why I called you and asked you to come home early!" Zelda cried. "I'm so sorry! I told them how valuable some of these things are, and how I'm not even allowed in here. I told them this room was totally off-limits and how mad you would be once you got back. But they forced me!" Zelda sniveled, crying fat crocodile tears. Malia had no idea she was such a skilled actress. "I tried to stop them, but there are three of them and only one of me!"

"What?" Bree was flabbergasted.

"That's not true!" Malia protested.

"We can explain," Dot said.

But Zelda's mom shook her head firmly. "That won't be necessary. I'm surprised at you. Who goes into someone's home and acts this way? Especially when you were hired to be there! What would your parents think?"

Even though it hadn't been their idea, Malia couldn't help but feel ashamed.

And then Zelda's mom said the worst thing of all. "Obviously, I cannot pay you after what took place here today. It goes without saying that we won't be needing your services anymore."

CHAPTER FOURTEEN
Dot

"**S**ometimes, our biggest challenges are actually our greatest blessings," said Dot's mom.

Dot wanted to take her mother's advice seriously, but it was very hard to do so when she was delivering it upside down.

Dot sat on the living room sofa, nestled amid a sea of brightly patterned pillows, while her mother hung, feet up, from some inane contraption that looked like an inverted treadmill. According to her, it was meant to promote blood flow to the head and (apparently) increase one's intuitive ability. According to Dot, it seemed like a great way to get a headache. It was just the latest thing her mother, a yogi–slash–tarot card reader–slash–Reiki master–slash–intuitive healer, was trying in the name of "self-care."

After what had gone down at Zelda's, Dot needed a little

motivational speech to get herself ready for the only babysitting job they had left: monster-sitting the Morris boys. Dot wasn't used to failing, and it felt like that was all she was doing these days. No matter how much they tried (and how much torture they had withstood), both Dot and Best Babysitters were holding on by a thread.

"I'm telling you, any way you look at it, these boys are like three little nightmares," Dot said.

"You know, Dot, you've been very fortunate that many things have come easy to you," her mother said, her words aimed at Dot's feet. "Perhaps the universe is presenting you with a challenge so you can work through some complicated feelings and get to know yourself a little better."

That didn't make any sense.

"I think I know myself just fine," Dot countered. "What I don't know is how someone who is only five years old can have so many issues."

Her mom may or may not have frowned at this. It was hard to tell because of gravity.

"Dot, everyone just wants to feel seen. Everyone just wants to feel cared for. Perhaps your job is to help these little boys feel like they're safe and that you accept them as they are."

Dot thought about this for a moment. "But what if I don't accept them?"

"Well, my love, maybe that's part of the issue."

Dot continued to mull over her mother's words as she, Malia, and Bree walked to the Morrises' House of Torture for the latest round of man-to-man combat with the five-year-olds. Was it possible that the problem was she didn't accept the boys? Dot considered this for a moment and then laughed. Of course she didn't accept them! These were kids who routinely did things like draw her coffin and threaten to light her on fire. How on earth was she supposed to feel? No amount of enlightenment could possibly stand up to the trio of terror. All she could do was hope that no one got injured, nothing got broken, and crying was kept to a minimum.

"WHAT'S THE SCARIEST THING YOU'VE EVER SEEN?" asked Smith when they arrived at the house.

Oh great, thought Dot. Apparently, it was time for this game again.

"Have you ever seen a shark?" asked Chase.

"HAVE YOU EVER SEEN A ZOMBIE?" yelled Smith.

"Have you ever seen a snake?" asked Chase.

"Have you ever seen a tarantula?" asked Clark, and put

something down on the kitchen table. It took Dot a second to register that it was, in fact, a tarantula. A rather giant, hairy, eight-legged tarantula. And it was very much alive.

As soon as she saw it, Bree screamed what was, quite possibly, the loudest scream that had ever been screamed.

"NOW YOU'VE SEEN ONE!" Smith cackled like a very mean hyena, which, the more Dot got to know him, the more she realized he basically was.

"That's Evelyn," said Chase, as the enormous furry arachnid slowly made its way across the kitchen table.

Bree screamed again.

"Does Evelyn have some sort of home she can go back inside of?" Malia asked, with a shudder.

"Perhaps," said Clark. "What do you want to give me for it?"

"I'm sorry, maybe I should rephrase myself. Please put Evelyn back in her cage NOW."

"EVELYN LIVES IN A TERRARIUM!" yelled Smith.

"I don't care what it's called, please put her back inside it!" said Dot.

With a huff, Clark reluctantly gathered up Evelyn's terrifying body and carried her back to his bedroom. The other boys followed close behind.

"I don't think I can do this today," Dot said, as soon as the boys were out of earshot. "My nerves are totally fried. I don't know what a nervous breakdown feels like, but I think I might be having one."

"Try to breathe. It's just another hour," said Malia. "We can put up with pretty much anything for an hour. Especially if we're together."

There was a time when Dot would have believed this. But then she met these three little boys and saw firsthand just how much destruction could take place in one hour. Before she could even reply, a demonic child voice beckoned.

"SITTERS! COME QUICK!" called Smith.

There is nothing like the alarmed cry of a child whose welfare you're responsible for to motivate a sitter to spring into action. All three girls jumped up and sprinted to the back door, where they were greeted by three panicked kindergarten faces. Luckily, they appeared to be unharmed.

"What's wrong?" asked Malia.

"WE NEED YOUR HELP!" screamed Smith. Dot realized that because Smith screamed about everything, it made his dramatic requests seem less urgent.

"There is a family of kittens trapped under the deck!" said Clark.

"Kittens!" said Bree, snapping to attention. Her favorite word had been spoken.

"Yeah! They're, uh, stuck under there," said Chase.

"THEY LOOK SAD AND HUNGRY," added Smith.

"We should take a look!" said Bree. Malia nodded in agreement.

"Have you ever seen these cats before?" asked Dot, who wasn't in the habit of approaching strange animals. "Are they from the neighborhood? Do you know if they live under the deck? Do they seem feral?"

"WHAT IS FERAL?" yelled Smith, unhelpfully.

"No, I've never seen them around here before," said Chase, with a shrug. "But they really do seem nice."

"Yeah," agreed Clark. "They seem like very nice cats."

"Okay, I guess we can check it out," Dot reluctantly agreed.

The boys hung back, staying up on the deck, while the girls made their way down the steps to get a better look at the kittens.

"They're over by the fence!" said Clark.

As it turned out, the only way to access the area underneath the deck was a narrow opening in between a couple of the boards. Bree, of course, was the first one to look inside.

"Awww, they're so cute!" cooed Bree.

"What do you see?" asked Dot.

"There's a mama and two—no, three!—babies," said Bree.

"I want to see!" said Malia.

"Hm. The mama is kind of stamping her foot," said Bree. "Is that normal?"

"I don't think it's normal for anything to stamp its foot," said Dot. "But if you let me take a look, I can tell you."

"Yeah, she seems kind of pissed," Bree confirmed. "And do cats have tails like that?"

"Tails like WHAT?" Malia reached the opening just before Dot did. Malia made a sound so shrill it was enough to send any animal into attack mode. She turned, horror written all over her face.

Dot gasped. The sight that greeted her was much worse than she imagined. "Oh, no. That's not a—" Before Dot could finish her sentence, the not-kitten sprayed a very terrible-smelling spray into the air.

"It's a skunk!" Malia yelled, staggering out of the way. But of course, it was too late. A cloud of horribleness surrounded them. The girls were already covered with skunk juice.

Malia made a choking sound.

Bree looked like she might pass out.

It was awful. Pungent and sour and completely overpowering. Dot wondered if she would ever be able to inhale normally again.

"Bree, how did you not recognize what a skunk looks like?" Dot said, gagging.

"I've never seen one before! And it was dark under there! Oh my god. I think I'm going to throw up," said Bree, covering her mouth with her hands.

"It smells like rotten eggs!" wailed Malia.

"THIS IS THE WORST THING THAT'S EVER HAPPENED TO ME!" Bree wailed. "WHAT KIND OF ANIMAL DOES SUCH A THING?"

Up on the deck, safely behind the screen door, someone laughed. It was an unnecessarily loud laugh, so it was probably Smith.

"You little shrimps!" Malia turned on them.

"We didn't know!" Clark held up his hands, defensively.

"We really thought it was a family of black-and-white kittens," said Chase.

"WE'RE FIVE! HOW WERE WE SUPPOSED TO KNOW THEY WEREN'T WEIRD CATS!" hollered you-know-who, followed by the sound of little feet scampering away and the *click* of the back door locking behind them.

As Dot stood there, delirious, exhausted, and covered in skunk juice, that *click* sounded like the final nail in the coffin for Best Babysitters. She wanted to remain hopeful. But she feared this just might be the end. Of their business, yes, and also of her sanity.

CHAPTER FIFTEEN

Bree

In the past few days, Bree had done a number of things she had never expected to do in her life. She had bathed in a tub full of tomato juice. She had showered using a weird mixture that her mother had made out of baking soda, vinegar, and dishwashing detergent, which smelled almost as bad as the skunk itself. She had spritzed herself with something called "miracle skunk solution" that Marc had ordered on the Internet. She had gone for many, many walks near windy bluffs in the hope that she could "air herself out."

Still, there was no denying the truth. Bree still reeked of skunk.

Her family members, while supportive, had tried to avoid sharing the same air space with her. Even Veronica, bless his sensitive feline nose, had made himself scarce.

Bree was smelly, and Bree was lonely. But most of all, Bree was sad.

Though she was slightly paranoid as to how others would react to the lingering scent of skunk, she was thrilled to have a reason to get out of the house and interact with actual human beings. Today, she and Chelsea were scheduled to meet with Bianca Salamanca again to discuss the reality of the salamander bridge.

Bree chose a particularly bright outfit—a hot pink shirtdress—figuring that maybe the hue would help distract from her odor. She also wore a couple of extra spritzes of Ariana's perfume, for good measure.

Once again, the meeting was at Bianca's office.

Chelsea was already there when Bree arrived.

"Have a seat, have a seat." Bianca gestured to an overstuffed brown leather club chair identical to the one Chelsea was sitting in. "We have much to discuss."

Chelsea sniffed the air. "I see you and Malia smell similarly," she whispered.

"I have some wonderful news!" Bianca held up a small stack of papers. "The estimate for the bridge is ready!"

This was so exciting! They were about to take the next step

in saving the salamanders. This was the one thing that was going to make all the effort worth it.

The pages had a very fancy-looking header for the firm of Melvin and Melanie.

Chelsea slowly flipped through the document as Bree looked on.

Blah blah blah plans . . . *blah blah blah concept development* . . . *blah blah blah square footage* . . . Where was the price?

Chelsea made her way to the final page and pointed to the bottom of the document. Then she gasped. Bree gasped, too. Her eyes nearly fell out of her head.

It was a very large number. It was so large, it involved a comma and more digits than any amount of money Bree had even dreamed of.

Who knew building an amphibian bridge could be so expensive? The amount Best Babysitters had set aside from their recent jobs wouldn't come close to covering the cost. Heck, she could babysit dozens more kids and it still might not be enough. This was impossible.

"What on earth . . ." Chelsea stammered. "How are we supposed to afford this? How can anyone, anywhere afford something like this?"

"That's actually quite reasonable!" said Bianca. "Given the circumstances, Mel and Mel did me a favor and extended a friendly discount."

"But we can't . . . And I could never . . ."

Bree had never seen Chelsea at such a loss for words.

Then Chelsea did the unexpected: She turned on Bree. "I told you we needed to be thinking bigger."

"What are you talking about? All of this is because of you!" Bree was furious. "The fancy bridge and the fancy ideas and the fancy price tag. You've turned this into some sort of competition to impress everyone in town instead of caring about the actual creatures you're supposed to be saving."

"Oh, please." Chelsea rolled her eyes. "If it were up to you, you'd be sitting on the side of the road selling brownies and manually scooping up lizards for all eternity."

"What are you two talking about?" Bianca was flabbergasted. "Is this amateur hour? Have you lost sight of what's important here? This is a once-in-a-lifetime opportunity to make a difference. This is the time to quit complaining, band together, and work."

Both girls fell silent.

"Sometimes you have to hold your nose—quite literally, in this case, as it really smells like skunk in here—and get stuff done." Bianca paced back and forth behind her desk. "Now, I don't want to hear another negative word out of either of you. And I do very strongly encourage you to accept the terms of this proposal. You can find a way to build this bridge. The life of every salamander in Playa del Mar depends on it."

Bree felt like she was in one of those movie scenes where the hero gets a pep talk from their mentor before they go off to save the world. The thing was, after the pep talk, you had to go save the world, and that was a lot of pressure.

"All right! Well, this has been a most productive meeting, but I have to get ready for office hours," said Bianca, signaling that Chelsea and Bree should make their exit.

"Thank you *so* much for all your help," Chelsea groveled. "You are so incredibly inspiring and we cannot tell you how much this means to us."

"Yes, thank you," Bree echoed, though her words came out sounding less dramatic than Chelsea's.

As soon as they reached the stairs outside Bianca's office, Chelsea's entire demeanor changed.

"What are we going to do?" she asked, in a clipped tone. "We need to act strategically."

"We do," Bree agreed.

"Oh my goodness, there is so much to do. I'm going to go

reach out to everyone I can! I'm going to call Ramona and all my connections at the Junior Future Leaders of America organization and everyone in my contact list!" Chelsea was speaking so fast she was practically vibrating. "You should work on brainstorming, too, and we can meet to discuss what we come up with! We have to act fast." And with that, she was off.

Bree walked across campus, Bianca's words still ringing in her head. She thought about what Bianca had said about working with people you don't like, and how that can sometimes be worth it to help the greater good. And that's when Bree had an idea.

The idea was either good or very, very bad. But she had a sneaking suspicion it might be her best idea yet. She couldn't wait to tell her friends.

"Oh, sweet universe, I've missed you!" said Malia, doing a spirited two-step along the tiled pathway that surrounded the mall's fabled food court. "Even though you have been oh-so-challenging, it is nice to be out in public again."

After the meeting with Bianca, Bree had sent a text to the group requesting a meeting.

It was the group's first public outing since the skunk incident. Though the scent hadn't totally faded, it had reached a point where it was somewhat acceptable for them to be in the presence of others. So, after a very long weekend spent in confinement, they decided to meet at the mall, where they could spend some time walking and browsing in addition to discussing business. Being around other humans (not to mention food and things that were available for purchase) seemed too good to be true.

Yet as they walked around the mall, Bree noticed that wherever they passed, strangers looked around, as if to see where the weird smell was coming from. One woman even followed them past five whole shops, making curious expressions and a few times even opening her mouth like she wanted to say something. But of course, no one was going to straight up ask them about it. It was a bit like when someone smells a fart and no one is willing to place the blame.

"I still can't believe this happened to us," said Malia, as one woman gave them a sidelong glance. "Of all the horrible babysitting gigs, the skunk incident had to be the worst."

Dot sighed. "I never thought I'd say this, but I think I'm just about done. I'm not sure I can do it again."

"What?" said Bree.

"I mean, not not go to the mall. I want to do that again. I just don't know if I have it in me anymore to keep fighting.

Like, what's the point? We try so hard and then we get skunked. Do we even *want* to do this anymore?"

"I hear you," Malia agreed. "I really do."

"Wait! No." Bree was indignant, not to mention a little surprised, to hear Malia's defeat. She wasn't ready to give up. Not on the salamanders, not on the fund-raiser, not on babysitting. Bree had come up with a plan.

She stopped in front of the toy store, which had brought her so much joy throughout her life. It seemed like the perfect place to say what she was about to say.

"I know that things have been a little tough lately. Okay, more than a little tough. Honestly, kind of terrible. We don't even have Zelda as a client anymore, and those weird little gremlins are all we have left. We're sad, we're tired, and we smell like skunk. But I know we can bounce back!"

Her friends just blinked at her.

"It may feel like the three of us can't possibly continue to do this anymore, but I have a plan where we wouldn't have to. Or, like, we would have to, but we could call in our secret weapon."

"Our secret weapon?" Dot looked more confused than ever.

"Zelda," said Bree.

"But we got fired from watching Zelda," said Malia.

"Not babysitting Zelda. Hiring Zelda. To help with the terrible trio."

Bree thought it was kind of a genius idea, and she hoped her friends would agree.

"Think about it," she urged. "Who understands the mind of a bully better than Zelda? No one. I bet she can outprank those pranksters like nobody else."

Dot frowned. "But what if they team up against us?"

"We'd have to make it worth her while not to. She's not going to be a sitter. She'll just be giving us advice. Like an evil genius for hire."

Dot looked intrigued. "It's certainly worth a try."

"We literally have nothing left to lose," agreed Malia.

"Great!" said Bree. "I'm glad you guys are on board with this, because I already texted her. She's meeting us in the food court in an hour."

CHAPTER SIXTEEN

MALIA

After a beautiful hour of mall roaming—culminating in zero purchases and just as many Connor Kelly sightings—the girls made their way over to the food court for the fated meeting. Right in front of Potato Jamboree, Zelda, dressed in a floral embroidered jacket Malia recognized from her mom's epic closet, was already waiting at a table.

Zelda sniffed the air. "What's that smell?"

"What smell?" said Malia, innocently.

"Do you guys really not smell that?" Zelda wrinkled her nose.

"We have no idea what you're talking about," said Bree, unconvincingly.

"It's like . . ." Zelda stopped and sniffed again. "Does somebody have eggs in their purse?"

"No," said Dot.

"I don't even like eggs," said Bree.

"I don't even like purses," said Malia.

"You guys are weird." Zelda rolled her eyes. "So why did you want me to meet you?"

"Because we have a proposition for you," said Malia.

"No," said Zelda. "My mom will never hire you back. It took hours to get the closet back in proper order, and she said one of her favorite lipsticks got smushed into a funny shape. I don't think she'll ever forgive you." She smirked triumphantly.

"It's not about that," said Bree. "We don't want to babysit you. Or be your friend. Or hang out with you—"

"You know what Bree means," Malia cut in, before Bree could describe any of the other activities they had no interest in sharing with Zelda. Their dislike was obviously mutual at this point, but there was still no sense in insulting her right before their big offer.

"One of our regular jobs is to babysit these three kindergarten boys," Dot explained. "And they can be a bit challenging."

"They're the worst!" said Bree. "Honestly the worst. Any bad thing you can imagine, they've probably done. Or are in the course of doing right now."

Way to sell it, Bree, Malia thought.

"And how is this my problem?" asked Zelda.

"The boys are notorious pranksters, and we want to outsmart them at their own game," said Malia. "If there's anyone who can help us, it's you."

Zelda narrowed her eyes.

"Let me get this straight. You want *me* to help *you?*" She considered this for a second. "Why on earth would I do that? It's pretty clear how I feel about you. And we all know I'm not really the babysitting type."

Malia took a deep breath. This wasn't going to be an easy sell. If they wanted to get anywhere, they would have to resort to flattery.

"Look, Zelda. We know you're a genius," she said. "Through the years, we may not have always been on the most enjoyable side of your genius, but anyone would have to admit that you're clever enough to come up with all sorts of plans that other people wouldn't have the ability to dream up."

Zelda seemed intrigued. "Go on," she said.

"Well, these little boys are sharp. Terrible, but sharp. And it's going to take a mind that's even better—a skilled expert —to outsmart them."

"And what's in it for me, exactly?"

"A cut of the revenue," said Dot.

"You wouldn't technically be babysitting, since we would be there, too. You'd really be operating on more of a consultancy basis," said Malia. She didn't know exactly what "consultancy" meant, but Ramona used the word a lot and it always sounded good.

"Okay," said Zelda. "How much are we talking?"

"We can give you a third." Malia paused to let that sink in. Zelda did not look impressed.

"Which is more than we would offer to anyone else in this scenario," Malia added. "We'll handle the actual child wrangling. You'll just give us your advice. Really, this is an excellent deal for you. After we split our share of the profit, you'd be making more than we would! We're willing to go so high because we think you're worth it."

Malia felt good about her negotiation skills. She had said all the right things and presented an offer that she thought seemed too good to pass up. Still, Zelda looked less than thrilled.

"I think I should be entitled to a majority of the wages for any job where my skills are that integral," she said.

"I'm sorry, WHAT?" said Malia. What was wrong with this person? What made her think she was entitled to most of the money? What did "integral" even mean? She should have known better than to try to do business with someone as unreasonable as Zelda.

Zelda blinked. "I won't go lower than half."

"Half?" Bree cut in. "Who do you think you are?"

Zelda was unfazed. "Take it or leave it."

"Fine," said Malia.

"What?" said Dot.

It was true that splitting their revenue with Zelda had not been part of the plan. But it wasn't forever. They were out of options. And desperate times called for desperate measures.

"Let's put those pranksters in their places," Zelda said, extending her hand.

Malia shook it. "We're excited to be in business with you," she said. She hoped the more she repeated it to herself, the more it might become true.

Zelda sniffed the air one last time.

"I swear, though, something really does smell funny."

CHAPTER SEVENTEEN

Dot

As the Best Babysitters plus their new consultant walked up to the Morris kids' house, it felt like they were a band of superheroes going to meet their nemesis. But secretly, Dot was a little excited. The time had come for Zelda to prove herself.

She couldn't wait to see how things would go down. Dot secretly hoped the boys would bring their collective A game, because if Zelda wanted half the wages, she had better work for them. And the scene when they arrived at the three terrors' house did not disappoint. Chase was wearing a ninja costume that was several sizes too big. Clark had chocolate smeared all over his face. Smith was panting, though she knew not why. It was probably better that way.

"Guys, this is our friend Zelda, who is going to be hanging out with us today," said Malia, like a kindergarten teacher opening up the floor for show-and-tell.

"I DON'T LIKE YOU," said Smith, though it wasn't clear to whom he was referring.

"Zelda is a weird name!" said Clark.

"Zelda is a video game," added Chase.

"WHY IS YOUR HAIR ORANGE?" asked Smith, at a volume that seemed even louder than usual.

Zelda, bless her troublemaking soul, didn't bat an eyelash. Instead, she reached into her tote bag and pulled out an airhorn—the kind people use at basketball games. And then she blasted Smith right in the face. It was a tactic that had never been used in these parts before. But this was a particularly dire moment in Best Babysitters history, so they were willing to roll with it.

"If you think that was loud, I'll show you loud," Zelda said.

Smith was so shocked, he didn't even have a comeback.

"Are you a referee?" asked Clark.

"Something like that," said Zelda. "I'm like a referee and a principal and a police officer and a witch. All in one."

"Wow," said Chase, "a witch."

"Can you fly?" asked Clark. "Do you have powers?"

"Yeah," said Zelda. "I know everything you're thinking."

Chase looked terrified.

"PROVE IT!" yelled Smith.

Zelda looked him square in the eye.

"I know about the water balloons," she said simply.

Smith looked shocked. Zelda's words had clearly struck a chord. Who knew if it was because Zelda had accurately read his mind or it was just a safe bet that all monster kids had some evil plan involving water balloons? Either way, Smith was a believer. Heck, at this point, even Dot was becoming a believer. She had no choice but to admit that Zelda's skills were impressive.

"I have an idea! How about a snack?" said Dot.

"SNACK! SNACK! SNACK!" chanted Smith.

She presented them with a big red plate piled high with carrot sticks, sugar snap peas, and a dollop of hummus, which their dad had left on the counter.

"GROSS!" yelled Smith. "I WOULD NEVER EAT THAT!"

"Yeah, we don't eat vegetables," said Clark, matter-of-factly.

"Me neither. I'm not allowed," said Chase.

"ORDER US FRENCH FRIES!" demanded Smith.

"We are not ordering French fries," said Dot.

"We are not ordering French fries," Clark repeated, in a gremlin voice.

"Are you a gremlin now?" asked Dot.

"Are you a gremlin now?" he parroted.

"Are you just going to repeat everything I say?"

"Are you just going to repeat everything I say?" Clark snickered at this.

"This is amateur," said Zelda.

"What?" asked Clark. "What is THAT supposed to mean?"

"See, I got you to say something else," said Zelda.

"Ugh!" snorted Clark, defeated.

"GOING TO THE BATHROOM! BE RIGHT BACK," said Smith.

"Don't," Zelda said, simply.

Smith stopped in his tracks.

"BUT I HAVE TO PEE!" he protested.

"Don't lie to me. I already told you I know about the water balloons. Do you think I was born yesterday?" Zelda turned to the other sitters. "He was going to get the bucket of water balloons they hid in Smith's room before we got here."

Clark's eyes grew wide. "You *are* a witch."

"WHAT!" yelled Smith. "HOW DID YOU KNOW THAT?"

"I know every game in the book, kid, because I practically invented them."

"DON'T CALL ME 'KID,' OLD WOMAN," said Smith, which was ridiculous, since Zelda wasn't even old enough to drive.

Zelda sounded the airhorn again. "What did I tell you about volume?"

"Sorry," said Smith, at a normal decibel level. It was the only time, in the history of their babysitting him, and perhaps in the history of his short life, that Smith had ever spoken at a regular volume. Never mind that the word he had just uttered was an apology. Zelda was a miracle worker.

They had expected Zelda to be good at predicting the monsters' actions, but this was next-level. This was like they'd hired a psychic wizard with four decades' worth of experience teaching kindergarten. To demons.

What sense did it make that Zelda—a loner with antisocial tendencies and a penchant for mischief—could have been so downright intuitive when it came to others? Perhaps, thought Dot, that was the secret to her particular brand of genius. Whatever it was, this was the magic ingredient they had been missing. With Zelda in their court, they could take on any job—even the worst of them—and know that it would be a success.

"That was seriously impressive," said Malia, as they left the Morrises' house two hours later. Malia counted out the bills from the boys' mom and handed Zelda her cut.

"I concur," said Dot. "I've been dealing with those demons for weeks, and you knew things about them I hadn't even begun to figure out."

"Yeah, how did you know about the water balloons?" asked Bree.

"Bree. A good babysitter never reveals her secrets." Zelda laughed as she pocketed her share of the money. "Anyway, I told you I was worth it."

Then she mimicked dropping an invisible mike, turned, and walked away.

CHAPTER EIGHTEEN

Bree

I've got you, salamander!" Bree said, kneeling by the side of the street and scooping the little creature up with one hand. She dodged away from the road in the nick of time, just as a kid on a bike zoomed past.

Bree panted, both exhilarated and exhausted. It was her best save yet.

"Great job!" said Chelsea, who was perched on a nearby tree trunk, typing away on her laptop. She reached out to offer Bree a high five.

"Meow," said Veronica, looking on from his cat carrier. If he was impressed by the save, he didn't let on.

Inspired by recent events, Bree was feeling many good feelings about their chances of raising money for the bridge. She had taken Bianca's words to heart, and she was finding it easier to work with difficult people (*ahem*, Chelsea) when the results seemed more than worth it. Each day that passed, they grew more committed than ever to building that bridge.

Today, she and Chelsea were meeting to get their game plan in order, and Bree was excited to share her ideas. (Even though she knew that no matter what she said, Chelsea would probably hate it.)

"So! I talked to Ramona about hosting a gala," Chelsea started off. "And we tossed around a bunch of ideas, including a seafood tower, a silent auction, and live entertainment in the form of dancing holograms of famous musicians from the past."

Bree was confused by a lot of this, but she let Chelsea continue.

"We think it's totally within the realm of possibility to pull all of this off. The question we're having is, who we really want to appeal to with our fund-raising efforts."

"We want to appeal to everyone!" Bree said. "Or at least, anyone who wants to help the salamanders."

"Well, yes. But do we want to attract big-ticket donors, or do we want to involve the community at large? Ramona was thinking maybe we make it more of a two-pronged approach. Appeal to the big donors for support, while hosting an event that's accessible for everyone. All ages, all interests . . . every-one."

"I'm so glad to hear you say that!" said Bree. "Because I think I have an idea."

"Yes?" Chelsea looked slightly afraid.

"Don't worry, it doesn't involve costumes," said Bree, as she checked for more crossing salamanders.

At that, Chelsea breathed a very audible sigh of relief.

"So, I know you weren't into the idea of my bake sale–slash–raffle," she started. "And you know I wasn't that thrilled with the idea of a big, fancy gala. But I think there is a way to combine the two into a formal—yet casual—fund-raiser."

"What do you mean?" Chelsea seemed curious.

"Well, if we combine forces, we can each use our strengths to make a fund-raiser that's the best of both worlds. We can still throw an event at the school, like I wanted to, but it will be a *much* bigger event than just a bake sale. We can still have all that stuff, like a bake sale and a craft fair and a raffle. But we can also contact local vendors and have them participate. And have live entertainment, to attract more of a crowd."

"Ooh! I like it," said Chelsea, adjusting the laptop in her lap. "We could have a taco truck and an ice cream stand. I can donate a college counseling session with me and my mom.

Maybe we can have a few different kinds of entertainment, like a portrait artist and a magician or something."

"And Marvelous Ray's can set up a carnival game with prizes!"

"And there can be pizza!" added Chelsea.

"And music!" said Bree.

"And dancing!" said Chelsea.

"Just no clowns." Bree was serious about that one.

"*Of course* no clowns," said Chelsea, typing at a furious pace. "This is great. I have so many ideas. I can ask Ramona for her advice! And, ooh! I can pitch it to my old internship coordinator at the local news! They love promoting community events. I bet they'd be thrilled to cover the story!"

"Oh my goodness, really? That would be amazing." The thought of the salamanders being covered on the news was almost enough to make Bree cry.

"Yes! I don't have her info on me right now, but let me run home and give her a call!" Chelsea jumped up from the tree trunk. "We don't have much time and I want to see if I can secure a spot as soon as possible!"

"Sounds great!" said Bree. "Keep me posted!"

With that, Chelsea hustled off to make her call, leaving Bree alone with her brain full of ideas. She felt really good about this fund-raiser, but she still wasn't sure how to take it over the top. She wanted it to be THE biggest event Playa del Mar had ever seen, something everyone would be thrilled to go to and would keep talking about for weeks.

But what would it look like? And more important, how would they make it happen?

CHAPTER NINETEEN

MALIA

Lunch. Today's meal involved something called cauli-flower rice, which was really just shredded-up cauli-flower that had no business calling itself rice. It sat in a bowl, where it was all mixed up with a sauce that had no business calling itself sauce. This was at least thirty percent more disappointing than the usual cafeteria fare. But Malia didn't care. The view more than made up for the disaster on her lunch tray.

As usual, Malia was practicing her favorite ritual: watching Connor Kelly float around the lunchroom looking impossibly good. Today, he wore a blue fleece hoodie that made him resemble a cross between an athlete and a cuddly lamb. It was easily one of his finest ensembles.

"Hi!" said Bree, ambling up to the table with her own

lunch tray. "Do you have any idea what this is?" She wrinkled her nose at the sight of the offending meal.

"It's cauliflower rice," said Malia.

"Why?" said Bree. "Just . . . why?"

Malia shrugged.

"Chelsea and I were able to get some new pledges for the salamander bridge fund-raiser," Bree reported.

"That's great!" said Malia, then held her tongue. She was happy about the new pledges, of course, but she would never be excited about any news involving Chelsea.

"We still have a ways to go. And we have to keep manning the crosswalk until we can build the bridge. But I just talked to Mr. Frang, and he said he's willing to offer extra credit to any environmental science students who sign up for a shift!"

Malia was genuinely excited by this news. Her environmental science grade left something to be desired.

A moment later, she saw a sight that was even more confusing than cauliflower masquerading as rice. Zelda—yes, Zelda—was approaching their lunch table. She placed her own tray down right next to Malia's. And then she took a seat.

Zelda had never so much as acknowledged them at lunch before, never mind sat at their table. Malia wasn't quite sure what to make of it. Malia was so confused by the events unfolding around her that she actually started eating the cauliflower rice.

She chewed in silence for a few moments. Bree looked at Malia, then back at Zelda, then back at Malia. She seemed to be equally confused.

"Uh, hi?" Malia ventured.

"Hi," Zelda said, taking a bite of her lunch like this was totally normal. "Isn't it so strange all the things they're trying to make with cauliflower these days?"

Malia wholeheartedly agreed with this statement—perhaps more than she had ever agreed with any words ever spoken—but she wasn't sure how to reply. Since when did Zelda act like her friend?

"My mom made a pizza the other night, and after the fact she tells me the crust was made of cauliflower," Zelda continued. "Like, what's next?"

"Yeah," Bree said, simply.

Malia dug into her own lunch. Because what else was there to do? A trio of French nannies had stolen all their business, everyone was obsessed with a bunch of amphibians, and now Zelda Hooper was eating lunch with them. The world was a bizarre and confusing place.

At least one thing remained the same, Malia thought while looking across the room to where Connor Kelly was making his way over to the drink vending machine.

Zelda looked at Malia, then to Connor, then back at Malia.

"Enjoying the show?" She smirked.

"I don't know what you're talking about," Malia said. It took all her self-control not to break out in the creepy grin she often made when she felt embarrassed.

Then Zelda leaned in, a little too close for comfort. "Why don't you go talk to him?" she whispered.

"What? Why would I do that?"

"Well, for starters, because it couldn't be more obvious that you want to," Zelda said.

"I do not," said Malia. Even though she did.

"Malia. You watch him like he's the only thing on television. It's not subtle." Zelda smirked again.

What was this noise? She had no idea she was being so obvious. Was everyone aware of her feelings for Connor? Even more horrifyingly, was *Connor* aware of her feelings for Connor?

Malia was at a loss for words.

Zelda continued. "Get that terrified look off your face.

There's nothing wrong with that. You're allowed to like some-body. There's a pretty good chance he likes you, too. The only annoying thing is if you don't do something about it."

"But . . . what would I do?"

"This is your LIFE, Malia. Make a move. Go say some-thing."

The thought made Malia want to faint into her cauliflower.

"What would I say?"

The thought of approaching Connor and saying multiple words to him—on purpose—was too much for her to handle. If he were to call her over, or ask her a question or something, then of course she would be happy to go talk to him. But Malia wasn't sure how forward she could be.

"You could start with 'hi.' Maybe ask him how his day is going," said Zelda.

"Isn't that weird?" asked Malia. "Why would I act like I want to know how his day is going?"

"Because you do."

Zelda was right. Malia always wanted to know how his day was going. Indeed, she devoted a sizeable part of her own day to wondering about it.

"But then he would know that I care!"

"Right . . ." Zelda looked skeptical. "But it's not like you're being super low-key about this. You're watching his every move. Wouldn't it be more direct to just ask him?"

Again, Zelda had a point.

"Go," she urged.

When a bully tells you to do something that's not totally horrible, you do it. So, Malia gingerly pushed her chair back and made her way across the cafeteria, legs shaking all the way. WHAT ON EARTH WAS HAPPENING? She had thought of this moment many times, but she hadn't planned on actually doing it. Malia told herself she could change direction at any time, but when she glanced back over her shoulder, Zelda was watching her intently. She had no choice but to continue walking—right up to Connor.

"Hey," said Malia, not smoothly. She was so nervous, the word sort of vibrated out of her mouth, like *he-eh-eh-eh-ey*.

"Hi, Malia," said Connor.

"How is your day?" She spoke softly, like maybe if nobody could hear her, this wasn't really happening.

"Huh?"

"How is your day going?" she said, a bit louder this time.

"Oh, you know," Connor said.

Malia didn't know. That's why she was asking. She also didn't know how to respond to that, so she just said, "Yeah."

"Yeah," repeated Connor, like some kind of adolescent parrot.

This was a complete disaster.

Malia took a deep breath.

Get ahold of yourself, said a voice inside her. *This is the subject you know best. You could talk ABOUT Connor Kelly for hours, so why not talk TO him? Think back on all the research you've done, and ask him about stuff he likes.*

"How is soccer going?" Malia asked.

"Good."

This boy did not make it easy.

"Have you heard about the salamander bridge?" she asked.

"Huh?" said Connor.

Apparently he had not.

"A bunch of us are trying to save the local salamanders that keep getting squashed by traffic. There's this section of Waveland Avenue where we set up a crosswalk, and Mr. Frang just announced that anyone who volunteers there will get extra credit."

"Oh, I should do that. I did so bad on the last quiz."

He had uttered two whole sentences. This was progress!

"We should go together!" Malia said. The words were out

of her mouth before she had a chance to realize what was happening.

"Yeah," said Connor.

"Great!" said Malia. "I'm doing the shift on Friday. Do you want to join? I'll put your name down. I'm helping Bree keep track of the sign-ups, so it's no trouble."

"Okay," said Connor.

"Great!" Malia said, again. Her brain couldn't think of other words, because SHE HAD JUST MADE A DATE WITH CONNOR KELLY. Was it a date? It was just extra credit. But it was happening at night. On purpose. Whatever —it was the closest thing Malia had ever had to a date, so she would take it.

"All right, so I guess I'll see you there," said Connor.

Malia nodded so that she wouldn't say "great" for a third time that minute. Then she turned and, in what she hoped was a smooth manner but knew was definitely not, started to make her way back to the table. No matter what Zelda had going on, Malia sort of owed it to her: This had suddenly become the most exciting day ever.

CHAPTER TWENTY

Dot

After the skunk incident, the girls had made a pact that no one, under any circumstances, would ever attempt to babysit the horrible boys alone. The official club rules had even been changed to include this fact. But somehow, the stars had misaligned, and now Dot found herself facing the monsters all on her own. Technically, though, she wasn't completely alone. Zelda would be there in spirit. And also on Dot's phone.

At the last moment, Bree got roped into watching her siblings (on the off chance that all three au pairs were already booked watching other families) and Malia was forced to accompany her parents to see evil Chelsea accept an award at a Future Young Leaders of America summit, hosted by none other than Ramona Abernathy. This had already resulted in many text message updates from Malia, who apparently felt tortured, invisible, and misunderstood. So Dot was forced to spend her afternoon with the furthest thing from young leaders: the trio of terrible boys.

The next-best thing to having backup was having virtual backup. So Zelda had agreed to be on call to offer advice (and Jedi mind tricks) whenever it was helpful.

Upon Dot's arrival at the boys' house, they decided to play a game called "zombies," which involved wandering around the house chanting, "Zombie! Zombie! Zombie!" over and over and occasionally walking into things. All things considered, it was actually one of the better things they'd played, as it was (not yet) destructive and involved minimal, if any, babysitter participation.

At some point, they tired of zombies and disappeared into Smith's bedroom. Dot knew they should probably be supervised, but they were playing quietly, so she decided to just let them do their thing. It wasn't often she got a moment of peace and quiet, and she was going to savor every moment.

"It's just a little poop!" said Clark, causing Dot to spring to attention.

"YEAH, WHAT'S THE BIG DEAL?" hollered Smith.

A very tearful Chase emerged from the bedroom. When

Dot asked what was wrong, she was met with silence, as Chase was seemingly the victim of a situation that was simply too horrible to mention.

Without meaning to, Dot found herself doing the deep pelvic breathing exercises her mother had taught her to combat stress. Once again, it was time to take this zoo to the playground, in the hopes of tiring them out.

"All right! Time to go outside!" said Dot.

"PARK! DARK! SHARK! LARK!" yelled Smith.

Dot already had a headache. The troop filed outside, taking the now familiar route to the very same park where the boys had wreaked havoc on so many days prior.

Dot placed an earbud in her ear and dialed Zelda as they approached. Out here in the open, she needed all the help she could get, and she wasn't taking any chances.

"Can you hear me okay?" asked Dot.

"Loud and clear," said Zelda.

"How's the background noise?"

"Well, I just heard Chase say, 'Your fart smells like cheddar cheese popcorn,' to one of the other boys, so it looks like we're pretty good," Zelda reported.

"Perfect!" said Dot.

"WHO ARE YOU TALKING TO?" yelled Smith.

"Nobody," Dot lied.

Dot entered the park, feeling good about the plan. Of course, the au pairs were once again holding court on the grassy knoll in the center of the park. All three of them were present, and they were joyfully leading the neighborhood children—Aloysius Blatt, Ruby and Jemima Woo, all three Gregory kids, and the Larsson triplets—in some very civilized game. They all held hands and stood in a big circle, walking slowly around and around.

"What are they doing?" asked Chase, wrinkling his nose in distaste at the sight of the other kids. Dot couldn't have agreed more.

"Tell them if they don't hit one another or set anything on fire, they'll get a treat later," said Zelda.

"Guys! If you don't hit each other or light any fires, there's a treat in your future!" Dot said.

"WHAT? NO FIRE?!" Smith was dismayed.

"What's the treat?" asked Clark.

"I can't tell you. It's a surprise," said Dot. "But I promise you'll like it."

"How do you know we'll like it?" Chase was suspicious.

"Tell them the witch read their minds and told you just what they'd like," Zelda supplied.

Dot did as she was told. The boys seemed satisfied. For that matter, so did Zelda.

Any time they got even a tiny bit rowdy, Dot would share that the witch could hear them, or the witch could see them, and the witch would know just what to do.

Miraculously, as the afternoon unfolded, the boys didn't make too much of a scene. Sure, they climbed and romped around and tussled with one another. It was a far cry from the slow-moving circle of silence taking place in the middle of the park. Still, compared to their usual antics, they were remarkably well-behaved.

"Are you ready for the treat?" Dot asked. The boys willingly climbed down off the playground and readied themselves for the walk home. The treat was that the witch—the real, live witch—was going to meet them back at Chase's house with ice cream pops.

The au pairs were talking to one another, and Dot had no idea what they were saying. As usual, their tone seemed mocking.

"Ugh!" Zelda reacted to whatever she had heard. "I have a message for the au pairs. Are you ready? I'm using a virtual translator."

"Uh-huh," said Dot.

"*Je comprends ce que vous dites,*" said a robotic voice. Dot did her best to repeat whatever the robot lady had said. Dot hoped her accent was good enough.

The au pairs looked up, shocked.

"We just told them that you understand what they're saying," Zelda explained. Who knew Zelda spoke decent French? This girl was full of surprises.

"*Depuis quand tu parles français?*" asked Genevieve.

"*Toujours,*" Dot replied, following Zelda's instructions.

"*Intéressant,*" Sophie replied. "*Alors pourquoi les familles ne vous embauchent pas?*"

The au pairs shared a hearty laugh about this.

"They're asking why, if you speak French, the families don't hire you instead of them," Zelda explained. And then added, "What a jerk."

"Because I don't need a gimmick," said Dot. "I'm just a good babysitter."

"Nice one!" said Zelda.

"Very well," said Claire. "Get back to your job, then."

And for once, Dot was happy to do so. She walked the little monsters out of the park, still on the phone with the big monster.

"That was fun!" said Zelda, who apparently enjoyed

manipulating people even from afar. "We should do that again sometime."

"Yes," Dot agreed. "That was far less painful than I expected."

"It's actually kind of fun to consult remotely," Zelda said. "Like being a puppet master. Or master of the universe."

"WE DIDN'T SET ANY FIRES!" yelled Smith.

"Yeah! What's the treat!" yelled Clark.

"Tell them to follow you," said Zelda, in her final command for the day. "The treat is waiting for them, at their house. I'll meet you guys there with the ice pops. But don't tell them anything until they see me."

Dot did as she was told.

Dot watched the boys take off running down the block. Maybe they weren't so bad after all, she thought. They were like any other little boys. Just with a little more energy, more action, more trouble. And she could handle that.

CHAPTER TWENTY-ONE

Bree

Marvelous Ray's said yes!" Malia yelled, at a volume so loud it rivaled even Smith Morris's. "They're up for donating a pizza booth, a prize display, and our choice of three of their most popular carnival games!"

At the news, the girls paused for an impromptu dance break. This lasted approximately thirty seconds before they returned to their stations to keep drumming up more support for the fund-raiser.

They were perched in various places around Bree's room, which had become command central for all things related to the big event.

"I think I'm closing in on a taco truck," Dot reported. "I'm waiting on one more email to confirm, but I have a good feeling."

"Excellent!" Bree made a note of this on her master document.

"Can we revisit why you're the one securing every business and donor in town?" Malia asked. "What is Chelsea contributing?"

"It's our two-pronged approach," Bree parroted what she had been told a million times before. "Chelsea is reaching out to the top-tier donors, and I am tackling the low-hanging fruit."

Malia made a face. "First of all, that sounds like something Ramona would say, and second of all, you are not tackling the low-hanging fruit. You are tackling all the fruit."

"Well, Chelsea is handling the press, including talking to some contact at the local TV station," Bree said, hopefully. "And if that comes through, that'll be a huge help."

"What's the status on that?" Dot asked.

"It's not confirmed yet," Bree reported.

Malia narrowed her eyes. "As I thought."

"The point is, right now everyone has to reach out to as many people as possible," Bree said.

"Well, you know, I talked to Connor," Malia said, trying—and failing—to hide her smile. "We're manning the crosswalk on Friday."

"We've heard," Dot said. "Once or twice. Or seventy times," she added under her breath.

"Do you think I can consider this a date?" Malia asked, with the face of a kid who really hopes her parents will let her keep the puppy.

"I think you can consider it extra credit," Dot said.

Malia's face fell. But then it brightened a moment later. "But he could have done extra credit with one of his friends, and he chose to do it with me. That means something."

"Definitely," Bree said reassuringly, making another check mark in the document.

Malia checked her phone and sighed. "I have to get home. It's my night to help with dinner."

Dot swung her backpack over her shoulder. "I have to get back, too. English paper. But I'll send a few more emails asking people to take shifts at the crosswalk."

"Amazing. Thank you!" Bree smiled. She was so glad to have her friends.

After her friends left, Bree went through her checklist. An awful lot of people had signed on to help, and they had made some great progress, but still. Bree couldn't stop thinking of the estimate from the eco-architects. That bridge was expensive

—a number with a comma and that many zeros didn't come easily. They would have to do even more.

"Meow," a tiny voice beckoned from somewhere under the bed.

That was it, the answer to all her problems.

Veronica!

Not cat Veronica. Person Veronica.

Maybe Bree could appeal to Veronica, a known animal lover, and tell her about the plight of the salamanders. All it would take was one teensy little performance and Bree knew they could easily raise enough money to build the salamanders the safest, prettiest bridge the world had ever seen.

Bree knew that maybe the odds of Veronica performing at the fund-raiser were kind of, sort of a long shot. But she also knew that Veronica was a good person who cared a lot about good causes, and that Chelsea wasn't the only person capable of appealing to really big donors.

There was just one thing left to do. Bree would have to write to Veronica.

She rifled around in her backpack and pulled out a piece of hot pink paper and a pen with ink that smelled like mango. For a moment, Bree felt a pang of sadness that she could no longer use glitter pens or glitter stationery or glitter stickers. But just as soon as the feeling came, it was gone.

Bree began to write.

Dear Veronica,

My name is Bree Robinson and I am thirteen years old and I am definitely your biggest fan.

I'm sure you remember me. We met recently in Playa del Mar when you gave a concert at the Arts Center. It was right near the porta potties and you were wearing amazing boots and I told you I named my cat after you. His name is Veronica and he is a big fan, too. Sometimes we listen to your music together and he howls, which sounds like it's a bad thing, but I promise it's good.

Anyway, I'm writing to you with a request. I know you love animals, and right now the salamanders need your help. It's their migratory season, and they're all trying to cross this one road in Playa del Mar, and it isn't going well. Salamanders like to travel at night, but they're small and kind of slow sometimes, and nighttime is dark, so it's very dangerous for them to cross the street. There are cars and bikes and trucks and scooters and sometimes even buses!

I thought we could build a bridge for them, and I

started doing things to try to raise the money. I became a salamander crossing guard to get donations, and dressed up like a salamander, and threw community meet-ups, and knocked on doors. But lizard bridges are really expensive. Like, REALLY expensive. I think if you could give a benefit concert here, even if it was for hardly any minutes, we could earn enough money to save the salamanders and make the world a better place.

Veronica, you are my only hope.

Please please please please please please please please please please please please help.

Love, your friend,

Bree

P.S. Please.

Bree looked down at the letter, pleased with herself. Her pride lasted for maybe forty-three seconds before she realized she had no idea where to send it. She didn't know how to mail something—how much did a stamp even cost? She also realized there was a good chance that since Veronica was always on tour, she might not see her fan mail for a very long time, if ever. The salamanders needed this bridge NOW. So Bree took a photo of the letter with her phone and posted it to Instagram, tagging Veronica. And she didn't stop there. She also sent it to her via direct message and emailed a copy to the official Veronica fan mail email address.

Bree sighed, satisfied with herself. Veronica was going to come through. This was the answer to everything. She knew Veronica wouldn't let her—and the salamanders, but mostly her—down.

CHAPTER TWENTY-TWO

MALIA

Malia vibrated through her day, unable to focus on a single thing. At lunch, she was so distracted that she accidentally mistook a cupcake-shaped rubber eraser that Shoko had put on the table for an actual cupcake, and attempted to take a giant bite out of it. She felt fully ridiculous, but forgave herself, because this level of nerves was to be expected. After all, this was the single most exciting day of her life thus far—the night of her date with Connor Kelly, to watch the salamanders cross the street.

Technically, she knew it wasn't a date. They just happened to be volunteering at the same time. But that was just logistics. What mattered was that this was a one-on-one hangout—in the evening hours—where Malia would get to experience more uninterrupted Connor Kelly time than ever before. It was reason for excitement.

All week long, she had stayed up late thinking through potential outfits and conversation topics. What would she say? What would HE say?

WOULD THEY KISS?

Just kidding. She knew they would never kiss. Malia didn't think she would be able to handle it, anyway. Her nerves might cause her to explode. Sometimes, though, when no one else was around, she would kiss her own hand and imagine it was Connor. For practice. Just in case.

Also just in case, she put on some of her favorite vanilla lip balm.

Then, with one final glance in the mirror, Malia was off.

She alternated between super-brisk steps (her nerves wanted her to move quickly) and slower ones (she needed to calm down). She had walked the streets of Playa del Mar hundreds of times before, but tonight, everything seemed a little brighter, a little more magical.

She walked past the grocery store and the library, where she had first had the idea to form a babysitting club–slash–business. She passed the playground and the weird green pond and the house that kept its Christmas decorations up all year long. Finally, she got to Waveland Avenue. Only three blocks stood between her and the rest of her life.

As she walked the final stretch, Malia felt like a character from one of the Shakespeare plays her language arts teacher was always forcing them to read out loud. In class, Shakespeare's prose never made any sense. Out here, under the moonlight, it still didn't make any sense, but Malia found herself thinking about it anyway.

And then, up ahead, she saw him.

HARK! she thought. It felt appropriately dramatic and romantic.

There he was. Sitting on a log, exactly where he was supposed to be. Malia sighed. He was so dependable. He looked upward, like he was gazing at the sky or thinking a deep thought or maybe just a little confused.

Malia ambled up to him.

"Oh, hey, Malia," Connor said.

"Oh, hey!" Malia hoped it sounded casual. "What a lovely evening! I mean, because of the weather. Of course. It's so nice outside, isn't it?" She willed herself to stop speaking.

"Yeah," said Connor. He scratched his head. "Do you, like, know what we're supposed to do?"

"Yeah, I know all about it!" Malia said, then feared she sounded too enthusiastic and therefore dorky, so she turned it down a notch. "I mean, yeah. I only know because Bree told me."

"'Kay," said Connor.

"We basically just watch out for salamanders, and if we see any, we scan for traffic and then hold up a sign so they can cross safely."

"'Kay." Connor nodded, and the hairs that made up his floppy bangs glistened under the starlight.

"Yeah," Malia said again.

For a few long moments, neither of them said anything. The sound of literal crickets sang in the night. Finally, Malia spoke.

"So. Lizards, huh?"

It wasn't her finest question, but at least someone was talking.

"Lizards. When I was little, I really wanted a pet iguana, but my parents said no."

Malia nodded excitedly. He was telling her stories from his life! This was amazing! This was everything she'd ever wanted. "Do you think maybe you'll still get an iguana one day?"

"Nah," said Connor, brushing his hair from his forehead. Two seconds later, it flopped right back to where it had been.

"Cool," said Malia.

"Yeah," said Connor.

There was another uncomfortably long pause. An owl—at least, Malia thought it was an owl—hooted from a tree somewhere.

A salamander appeared near the side of the road. It looked skittish and confused. Malia silently thanked it for existing.

"Is that one of them?" Connor asked.

"Yeah," said Malia.

They scanned the street for traffic. No one was coming, in either direction, so the amphibian meandered across without any complications. So far, this was pretty easy.

"I really like animals," Malia said. "That's why I wanted to do this." She thought it sounded like a nice, wholesome thing to say. Of course, her motivation for being there that particular night had very little to do with animals, salamanders or otherwise. But there was no reason Connor needed to know that.

"Oh, that's nice. I'm not really that into lizards anymore," said Connor. "I just wanted the extra credit. And I guess, like, nobody deserves to get squished, you know?"

"Of course not." Malia nodded in agreement.

She felt like she might burst. Connor Kelly. So caring. So sensitive. So in touch with the plight of all beings.

"You know, we're planning a big fund-raiser to raise money for the salamander efforts," Malia said. "It's going to be on the field at school, and there will be food and games and raffles and stuff to buy, and maybe even a concert. You should totally come. With Aidan and Josh, of course." She paused, suddenly afraid she was rambling. "I mean, not because you care about the salamanders that much, but just because it will be a fun time." She wished he would suggest that maybe they go together.

"Yeah. I'm kinda hungry," Connor said instead.

"Oh! We could, like, get a grilled cheese or something?" Malia suggested. If they shared actual food together, that would make it more like a date.

"Yeah!" Connor said.

"Great!" Malia said.

"Is it cool if we leave the lizards, though?" Connor asked.

"Oh, right," said Malia. She'd momentarily forgotten about the point of this entire evening. "Yeah, I guess we'd better not go anywhere."

They grew quiet again, and the crickets continued doing

their thing. Then Malia decided to unleash her secret weapon, which she had been saving for the right moment.

"Actually, if you're hungry, I think I might have some sunflower seeds in my bag?" She very much knew the seeds were in her bag, because she had very intentionally packed them. She had watched Connor eat sunflower seeds during study hall approximately four thousand five hundred twenty-eight times, and she wasn't going to let that knowledge go to waste. Maybe, she reasoned, if Connor thought they shared a favorite snack, he might recognize that Malia was his soul mate.

"That's so weird! My mom always buys sunflower seeds, too," said Connor.

Not exactly the reaction she'd hoped for, but Malia would take it.

As Malia handed off the seeds, one of his fingers brushed hers. She thought she might die.

The sound of his chewing was beautiful. Malia wished she could tell him how she felt about him—all the days she'd spent semi-creepily watching him move throughout the school, all the times she'd thought about him, all the things she admired about him and ways she found him cute and funny and endearing and amazing and sweet and so totally unlike anyone else.

"I thought there would be more lizards," she said instead.

Her phone buzzed. It was a text from Zelda. Malia was afraid to look at it, in case it said something mean. Or in case it was something she wouldn't want Connor to see. Or really, in case it said anything at all.

How's it going?

What was this? Malia looked around, in case it was some kind of trick. She wouldn't be surprised if Zelda popped out of the bushes with an entire camera crew and announced that they were on a show about one-sided crushes.

It's fine, Malia cautiously responded.

Good. Glad to hear it, Zelda replied. **Remember, this is your life. Don't be afraid to make a move.**

Malia slipped her phone back in her pocket, so as not to get too distracted from watching the road. Having Connor in her line of vision was already distracting enough.

Malia wanted to be the kind of person who could make the first move. But how did you know when it was the right time? How did you know when the person next to you found you more interesting than lizards, which they didn't even really care about anymore?

"So, about the salamander fund-raiser," Malia said. "I'll definitely keep you posted when I know more about the games and the prizes and who's coming and stuff."

"Sounds good," said Connor.

"Um, maybe I could—" She noticed her arm was actually shaking. This was absurd. She willed it to stop with every fiber of her being. "I could, like, give you my number."

OH MY GOODNESS, WHAT DID I JUST SAY?

"Sure," said Connor. He reached into his perfect Connor-y jeans pocket and pulled out his perfect Connor-y phone.

Over the next few blessed minutes, the unthinkable occurred. Connor typed a series of numbers—MALIA'S OWN PERSONAL TELEPHONE NUMBER—into his phone WITH HIS PERFECT CONNOR-Y FINGERS. The very same fingers that dribbled basketballs and carried lunch trays and slipped ever so casually into his jeans pockets had now encountered her phone number.

HOW WAS THIS REALITY?

"Oh." He furrowed his brow and looked at his phone with a confused expression.

WHAT COULD IT MEAN?

"It's already in here," he said. He held up his phone, where, sure enough, "Malia Twiggs" was already programmed into his contacts.

How was this possible? Connor Kelly already had her number! Had she given it to him? Where had it come from? And yet, he had never used it. She wasn't sure how to feel about this newfound knowledge.

"Weird," he said, with a resigned shrug.

"Yeah, really weird," Malia confirmed.

"Well, I'll text you," he said, holding up his phone with one hand and making a typing gesture with the other, like there might be some sort of confusion as to what he meant. Then they fell back into silence, leaving Malia to process all that had just happened.

She knew that, at the end of the night, there would be no kiss, or even a good-night hug. But this had already far exceeded her expectations. Connor Kelly had sat right next to her for many minutes in a row. He had taken her number. Again, apparently. But this time she would remember giving it to him. She would remember this entire night forever. She hoped it would never end.

CHAPTER TWENTY-THREE

Dot

I'M HUNGRY!" whined Smith.

Dot and Zelda were currently herding the monsters around town, which meant Zelda was more or less controlling them, while Dot offered some assistance, in terms of both manual labor and emotional support.

"I'm hungry, too!" said Clark.

"Me too!" echoed Chase.

"GIVE US FOOD!" yelled Smith.

It was the latest of the many requests they had made that day, including wanting to collect every bug they'd passed, asking to use every public toilet, attempting to talk to multiple strangers, and bombarding the sitters with questions like, "Why do cheeses make such weird farts?" At least this need was simple enough to attend to.

"I've been wanting to go to the patisserie," said Zelda, looking to Dot. "Should we take them there?"

Of course, thought Dot. No one was immune to the wonder of freshly baked French pastries. Not even Zelda Hooper.

Before Dot even had a chance to respond, they had their answer.

"YEAH! I WANT A PAN-O-CHOCOLATE!" yelled Smith.

"Yes!!!! Best stuff EVER!" agreed Chase.

While the boys' behavior had vastly improved in Zelda's presence, Smith's volume had not. Dot could only imagine how much it was likely to increase after he'd consumed sugar.

"Okay, then, let's go check it out," Dot said.

She was willing to go along with this plan, but as a matter of pride, Dot would still abstain from anything even remotely related to the au pairs — including the eating of delicious pastries. Yet as they approached the little bakery, the intoxicating aroma was determined to change her mind. That smell. Oh, that smell. It was the most delicious smell in the entire universe.

Dot felt conflicted. She didn't want to like the *pain au chocolat* as much as she did. But ever since that first bite, it had haunted her. It was like a croissant with an overwhelmingly pleasant chocolately surprise inside. It was like bread and cookies had had a baby. It was the best use of carbohydrates she'd ever encountered.

Through the shop's front window, Dot saw Sophie, Genevieve, and Claire (alone, *sans* babysitting charges) sitting at a café table, sipping coffee—*What non-adult drinks coffee?* she thought—and picking at a plain croissant. In their assortment of flouncy blouses, cool cropped jackets, and artfully disheveled hair, they looked like something out of a catalog selling an impossibly chic life. In fact, the entire place was impossibly chic, from the teeny café tables and perfect latticework chairs to the little flower-filled vases adorning every tabletop.

"Why don't you go in and place the order while I stay outside with the boys," said Zelda, peering in the window. "Otherwise, I can't imagine how many tiny glass things they'll find to break in there."

Dot couldn't decide which was worse—staying here and wrangling the monsters or going in and confronting the enemy. But she reasoned the boys would be better behaved in Zelda's presence, so she was willing to take one for the team.

"Okay," said Dot. It was, quite possibly, the least enthusiastic she had ever sounded.

"Ooh! I know," said Zelda. She rummaged around in her canvas tote bag and pulled out her earbuds. "Put one of these in. I'll listen to your conversation from out here, and I'll feed you lines like we did the other day in the park."

Dot was skeptical. "What if they notice?"

"They won't. Don't worry! It'll be fun."

Dot placed the earbud in her ear and pushed through the adorable front door. The smell of pastry was even more intoxicating on the inside. The air was literally delicious.

As Dot walked up to the counter to place her order, Genevieve said something apparently funny and all three sisters threw their heads back in laughter. Was it possible that even laughter sounded better in French?

That's it, Dot thought. The chocolate croissant had haunted her long enough. She was going to order one after all. Besides, eating a pastry was the least she could do to lift her spirits after taking in the current scene.

She ordered five in total—one each for the boys, herself, and Zelda—and handed the counter attendant the money. She was just turning to leave, hands gripping a paper bag full of carbohydrate goodness, when a superior voice summoned her over.

"Oh! Hello, Dot," said Genevieve.

"*Bonjour, mes amies.*" Dot repeated exactly what she heard in her ear.

"*Oh là là! Je vois que tu parles français maintenant,*" said Sophie.

"*Effectivement. Je te vois sous-estimé mes capacités,*" Dot replied. She had no idea what she was saying, but she felt great about it. Before the au pairs had a chance to respond, another phrase rang out in her earpiece. "*J'aime péter,*" Dot repeated exactly what she'd heard, even though it wasn't her turn to speak.

The computerized voice spoke again, repeating the same phrase.

"*J'aime péter.*" Dot said it again.

The French girls shot her a curious look, then burst into laughter. Yes, that settled it. Laughter definitely did sound better in French.

"*Mon gaz sent bon,*" Dot said, following the translation. Why did Zelda have her talking about gas? "*Très, très bien. Le meilleur gaz sur la planète.*"

"WHAT?" said Claire, exploding into giggles.

"What is wrong with you?" asked Genevieve.

Dot was lost. Something had gone horribly wrong, but she knew not what.

"You like to fart? And your gas smells good?" Sophie laughed.

"The best gas on the planet!" said Claire, hyperventilating from laughter.

"*Je suis le seigneur du mal,*" said the voice in Dot's earbud. She had no idea what it meant, but after what just went down, she didn't dare repeat it.

Dot felt her face grow hot. She'd just made a complete fool of herself. She turned and glared daggers at Zelda, who stood in the front window, making funny faces and gesturing wildly. Now she was making fun of Dot, too?

Understanding crashed over her. Zelda hadn't turned over a new leaf at all. She was still up to her same old tricks, humiliating everyone and deriving a sick pleasure from it. Dot couldn't believe she'd let down her guard. How did that old saying go? "Fool me once, shame on you. Fool me twice, shame on me." Zelda had fooled them all more times than anyone could count. And all Dot felt was a terrible amount of shame.

CHAPTER TWENTY-FOUR

Bree

I love you more than dinosaurs, more than dino-dino-dinosaurs," sang Bree.

"Meow," said Veronica.

"*I will give you all my roars, more than big Tyrannosaurs,*" she sang.

"Meow."

This was Veronica's favorite Veronica song.

Sometimes, Veronica liked when Bree sang to him. Actually, she wasn't totally sure this was the case, but he clearly didn't hate it, or he would have made that known. In any event, Bree enjoyed singing to Veronica, so she continued to do it. It made her happy, too.

Bree still hadn't heard back from the other Veronica about playing at the fund-raiser, but she was a very busy pop star. Bree knew it was only a matter of time.

Bree was just getting to the chorus when she heard panicked cries from downstairs.

"Bree! Come see this!" Bailey yelled. Whatever it was, it sounded urgent.

Bree raced down the plush carpeted stairs and into the family room. The large-screen TV was tuned to the local news, where they were covering the Save the Salamanders campaign. Chelsea's contact had come through!

Bree settled in front of the TV. This was so exciting! Though Bree hadn't heard back from human Veronica, Marvelous Ray's had signed on to be an official sponsor of the salamander fund-raiser. And now this! Bree couldn't wait to see the segment.

LOCAL SALAMANDERS IN DANGER, read the headline at the bottom of the screen. A video clip showed a spotted salamander walking slowly across the road.

"As it turns out, hundreds of these little guys are in danger from being killed by oncoming traffic. But luckily, citizens are taking steps to change that," said a female reporter.

"This is amazing!" said Bree. Her cause was getting top billing on the news! Now her family would see what a difference she was making! And maybe more people from the community would want to get involved!

"Now we'd like to introduce you to the local hero who brought all this to light," said the reporter. *Huh?* Bree thought. No one had interviewed her. Bree's heart stopped beating as the screen changed to a very disturbing image. It was Chelsea's giant face, and it was beaming.

"This brilliant and courageous young woman, at only seventeen years old, has proven to be quite the animal activist," said the reporter.

OMG.

Chelsea continued smiling from inside Bree's family's TV.

A local reporter held a microphone up to Chelsea's face. *LOCAL GIRL SAVES SALAMANDERS*, read the ticker at the bottom of the screen.

What was this noise?

"Well, one day I was crossing Waveland Avenue in the early evening, and I saw a salamander get hit by a bike," Chelsea said. "It was really upsetting. Then I saw another one, which led me to research the salamanders' migratory patterns."

Huh? This was Bree's story! Chelsea had stolen her story, and now she was taking all the credit for Bree's work. What kind of person did such a thing?

Chelsea prattled on. "I realized that dozens of these animals were being harmed right here in our community, and it seemed like something had to be done." She stared straight into the camera, a look of pure bravery flashing across her face. Bree was anti-violence, but she had the urge to leap at the TV and kick it with all her might. "So I decided to start a movement to make a difference. And what a difference it is making. I'm currently planning a huge fund-raiser at the Playa del Mar school, and everyone in the community is invited!"

"What a brave and inspiring young woman," said the reporter.

"Oh, for goodness's sake," Bree grumbled, rolling her eyes at the TV.

The display at the bottom of the screen changed to read, *HIGH SCHOOL STUDENT TURNED SALAMANDER SAVIOR.*

"Wow," said Bailey, looking at the TV with awe. "That's who's saving the salamanders? She's awesome! What's she like in person? You're lucky you get to work with her."

"She lied," Bree said softly. "None of this was her idea. I'M THE ONE SAVING THE SALAMANDERS!" Now she was fired up.

"But the TV just said that *she* was saving them." Bailey pointed at the screen.

"It's a lie!" Bree repeated. "She's just trying to take all the credit."

"Oh. Then that is too weird," Bailey agreed. "You should do something! Call the news and tell them it was really you!"

Bree supposed she could, but she wasn't sure how much good that would do. The segment was over. It had already run. Chelsea had already lied to her, and now she had also lied to the world. In the end, Chelsea didn't really care about creating excitement or raising money—or even about saving salamanders. She only cared about getting recognition. Malia had been right.

Still, Bailey had a point. Bree had to do something. So she picked up her phone and called the only person deserving of her anger: Chelsea.

"Hello?" Chelsea answered, with an impossible amount of glee in her voice. Bree could picture her flipping her hair as she spoke.

"I'm sure you just saw the local news segment," said Bree.

"Yes! Wasn't it fabulous?" Chelsea gushed. "The camera captured my bad side, but overall I think it was really great and hopefully lots and lots of people saw it!"

"Don't you think you forgot to mention something really important?" Bree's heart was beating so fast that she could barely get the words out.

"Hmm." Chelsea paused. "I mentioned the event. I talked about the cause. I mentioned all the major plot points of how the movement came together. So, no, I don't think I forgot anything."

"YOU FORGOT ME!" Bree was surprised, and a little bit proud, that she could demonstrate such rage. "You acted like the story was your story. You acted like you've done everything yourself. This entire organization was my idea and I've been doing all the legwork for the fund-raiser, and you didn't mention me once!"

"Bree." Chelsea sighed. "I understand you have very limited experience with broadcast journalism, so it's perfectly understandable that you don't get this, but when you're addressing an audience, it's important that you keep the story simple and don't convolute it with unnecessary details."

"I AM A PERSON," Bree wailed. "I AM NOT A DETAIL."

Bailey, who was still in the room watching this whole thing go down, looked at her with very wide eyes.

"You're obviously very upset right now, but I'm sure with

some amount of distance, you'll see that I was only doing what was best for the cause." Chelsea spoke in the same exhausted tone Bree's mom used when everyone in the family was acting up at once.

Furious, Bree hung up the phone. She supposed she was glad that she'd stood up for herself, but the conversation had left her feeling even more frustrated.

Bree knew the important thing was the salamanders. And now that the cause had gotten some attention, maybe it would inspire more people to get involved. The best use of her time and energy was planning the big salamander fund-raiser. It was going to be a huge success, and the credit would be hers and hers alone.

But that didn't help the fact that it felt so bad.

CHAPTER TWENTY-FIVE

MALIA

Malia trudged down the street even slower than a sala-mander on a hot summer's day. Bree and Dot weren't much better, plodding along beside her. They were all headed to the Morrises' house, and the dread was so palpable, it was as if their bodies wanted to delay their arrival as long as humanly possible.

"I'm sad," said Bree. "How will I ever trust anyone again? Chelsea took all the credit for my ideas. It's like, why bother putting so much effort in when we live in a world that doesn't have any values?"

"I won't say I told you so," said Malia.

"You kind of just did," said Dot.

"Well, we already knew Chelsea was the worst ever," said Malia. "And I'm sad, too. What if we never get any of our old business back? Is this all there is? Is life destined to be nothing but school and the three monsters for the rest of forever?"

If Malia was being perfectly honest, there was something else making her sad: the part where Connor still hadn't texted her yet. She had taken to looking at her phone a few times a day—okay, a few times an hour. Okay, whenever it occurred to her, which may have been even more often than that. But his name never popped up. She was losing hope.

"Honestly, just walking to Smith's house would be reason enough for sadness," said Dot. "But I'm sad about both of the things you guys mentioned, and also that I let Zelda prank me again at the patisserie. And that the au pairs aren't very nice. Why do good things happen to people who don't deserve them? Is karma not real?"

The three of them let out a collective sigh.

"And here we are," said Malia, as they arrived at the Morrises' driveway.

"The saddest place on earth," said Bree.

"And it's going to be even worse without Zelda here to be a monster-whisperer," said Dot.

"I can't believe she double-crossed us," said Bree.

"That's just what she does," Malia huffed. "She's been

doing it to me ever since we were toddlers. Why would she stop now?"

The front door opened. Malia expected the usual greeting —one of the boys, dressed as a gremlin, holding a lit match. But instead, it was their dad. And he looked peaceful.

"Oh, hi, girls!" he said. "I had no idea the whole team was planning to show up. Didn't you get the message?"

What message?

"No," said Malia. "Do the boys not need sitting today?"

"They do, but we won't need all four of you! They requested that only Zelda watch them." And as if on cue, Zelda appeared in the front hallway, grinning back at them.

WHAT? thought Malia. It didn't make any sense. After what had happened at the patisserie, the girls had decided that they had to call off their arrangement with Zelda. They hadn't told her about this job, yet here she was.

"Wait, what are you doing here?" asked Malia.

"I'm watching the boys on my own. I'm their new exclusive babysitter." She shrugged, like taking over the only remaining business in town was her final prank. "They specifically requested that 'only the witch' watches them from now on." She gave a little chuckle.

Mr. Morris smiled.

"They've really taken a liking to this one!" he said, then disappeared from sight.

Malia wanted to hurl.

"I'm sorry, but if you'll excuse me, I really should get back to the task at hand," Zelda said. "I guess I'll be seeing you later!" And with that, she closed the door in their faces.

To Malia, it felt like a symbolic door had just closed as well.

"'Only the witch'?" Dot repeated, screwing her face up into a scowl.

"At least we don't have to spend the day with demon spawn," said Bree. "And we can spend this time planning the fund-raiser!" Though even she seemed barely comforted by that thought.

"That's one way of looking at it," said Dot.

But Malia couldn't see a bright side. They had arrived at a point where there was no bright side. Their only job—a job they hadn't even particularly wanted—had disappeared right before their eyes. What did they have left? The business was officially over.

CHAPTER TWENTY-SIX

Dot

"I cannot believe we're here. Doesn't it feel a little like supporting the enemy?" Dot said, while taking a hearty bite of a *pain au chocolat*. She looked back and forth across the patisserie, searching for any glimpse of the enemy.

"Are they still the enemy if they've won?" asked Malia. "At that point, it's more like they're just the winner. And we are the sad people. Who have given up."

"What now?" asked Bree, unrolling a pastry that looked like a very complicated bow.

"So! I was thinking. Since there are no children left, maybe we can still babysit for other things," Malia offered.

"Things . . . besides babies?" asked Dot.

"Yes, like plants! We could water them when people go out of town. And they don't talk, so offering additional language skills will never be an issue," said Malia. "Dot, remember that one time you plant-sat? That was pretty easy, right?"

"Um, yes, I do remember, and no, that's absurd," said Dot. "Plant-sitting is not a marketable skill. Plus, how much could we charge for that? Watering someone's cactus for three seconds is very different than spending an entire afternoon with someone's children."

"Okay, well, we could get into pet-sitting." Malia was really trying here. "We could charge different prices for pet-sitting and dog-walking and, uh, whatever other services animals require. Maybe we could learn to groom them."

Even Bree, the world's preeminent lover of pets, wrinkled her nose at this idea. "I already have my hands full with pets," she said. "Between Veronica and the salamanders, I couldn't possibly give my full attention to any more animals right now. Plus, that's not our specialty! That's not why we got into this."

"Pet grooming is an entirely separate career," Dot argued. "One that I, personally, have zero interest in pursuing. Plus, pet hair is even worse than lint, you know. And I wear an awful lot of black." She smoothed her hands over her black T-shirt to make her point.

Bree nodded solemnly. "Dog grooming is a very serious

thing, not to be taken lightly." She paused before adding, "Especially in Japan. Artistic dog grooming is *huge* in Japan."

"All right, then. No grooming. But it might be smart to still consider pet-sitting. Occasionally." Malia sighed.

"Where is this coming from?" asked Bree. "Do you really think we're done with babysitting forever? You've never been one to back down when the going gets tough. So why now?"

"Because I don't see any way out," said Malia. "First we had to contend with the Seaside Sitters, and then our own employees started to take all our business, and now this? How many more times is this going to happen?"

"Probably infinitely more times, because competition is an unavoidable part of business, especially in an open market," said Dot.

Malia shot her a pointed look.

Bree looked at her like she was speaking Swahili.

"Right, that," Malia said. "Plus, even if I were trying to remain positive, the fact stands that there are no jobs left," she concluded. "NO JOBS. NO MONEY. The jig is up. I'm tired. I feel like I've already given an entire lifetime's worth of work. And we haven't even started high school yet!"

"I know the feeling," said Dot. "I feel remarkably burnt-out."

No sooner were the words out of her mouth than the shop's front door opened and in walked the enemy—all three of them.

She had no idea what they were saying, but she could make out the sound of their names.

"*Oh, regardez, c'est* Dot. *Cette* babysitter *américaine inefficace. Et* Malia *et* Bree, *qui sont tout aussi mauvaises*!" Then they burst into a cloud of hearty laughter.

Dot didn't have the tools to provide a well-timed zinger, but she didn't care. She had no desire to insert herself into this conversation. She had given up. Let the au pairs have their gossipy conversation. Let them have their growing business and their delicious pastries and their outfits that looked effortlessly chic. Let them have it all. Letting go was easier than caring.

CHAPTER TWENTY-SEVEN

Bree

"**D**oes this *A* look wonky?" Dot asked, frowning.

Bree squinted. It wasn't the most beautiful *A* she had ever seen, but it was good enough.

"It looks great!" she said, because Veronica's cat therapist had taught her that positive reinforcement was very important.

The girls were gathered at Bree's house, where they were hard at work on signage for the Save the Salamanders fundraiser. There were signs for each booth, signs for the food stations, a map of the festivities, and a giant banner (with the questionable letter *A*).

"How is Chelsea these days?" asked Malia, painting a *D* that Bree had to admit looked quite artful.

"You're the one who lives with her!" said Bree.

"But I avoid her as much as possible," Malia said. "Also, I

don't mean how is she doing in life, I mean, how has she been after the whole news fiasco?"

"Honestly, I haven't heard from her," said Bree. "I imagine she's running around taking credit for everything, including the *D* you are currently painting."

Malia laughed.

"For what it's worth, it will be wonderful event," said Dot. "And everyone who counts knows you are the heart of this operation."

"Aw, thanks," said Bree.

Bree was still upset about what had happened with Chelsea, but she was doing her best to "soldier on," as her mom would say. The day of the fund-raiser was almost here, and all her energy needed to go toward making sure it was the best event ever.

If Bree was being honest, the thing that was bothering her the most at this point wasn't Chelsea. It was that Bree still hadn't heard from human Veronica.

She knew that it might be silly to hope for a miracle. After all, Veronica was a super super super super famous star with a mega-packed schedule and a gazillion important events to attend. But Bree still had hope she would come through. She would just keep hoping until she felt like she might burst.

"I hope everyone comes to the event," said Bree.

"They will!" Malia said.

Bree hoped Malia was right. After everything everyone had done, she just hoped they would raise enough money to build the bridge. Then all of it would be worth it.

Later that morning, the Robinson family was gathered in their living room for what Bree's mom liked to call "family time." This typically meant everyone just sat in a room together and individually stared at their phones. Today, Emma was coloring. Olivia was taking turns putting each of the crayons in her mouth when no one was looking. Bailey was engrossed in an iPad. Bree's mom and Marc were watching the local news, while absently scrolling on their devices.

Bree was focused on her homework, not paying much attention to everything else going on around her. She enjoyed family time, because it was just so nice to be around people while doing icky things like geometry.

"Isn't that the bakery Sophie's parents own?" asked Bree's mom.

Bree looked up, where Jolie Pâtisserie was, in fact, on the news.

"Uh-huh," she said, her eyes now glued to the screen.

HEALTH CRISIS AT POPULAR EATERY, read the headline at the bottom of the screen. The camera was stationed outside the patisserie, with its red-and-white-striped awning flapping in the wind in the background. But that wasn't the most surprising thing. No, the real surprise was Zelda's face, which was now prominently displayed on the screen. She stood in front of the bakery, where she appeared to be having some sort of meltdown.

"I'm here at Jolie Pâtisserie, where it appears that salamanders—the very same salamanders that have been receiving so much attention of late—have apparently been making appearances in the kitchen," said the reporter. The woman turned to Zelda and held her large microphone up to Zelda's very dismayed-looking face. "Can you tell us what happened?"

"I was just sitting here eating a *pain au chocolat*, and I looked down to see that there was a very obvious lizard footprint in the *chocolat*," Zelda said, with a convincing amount of terror. She held her pastry aloft in one shaking hand. The camera zoomed in to where, indeed, a tiny lizard foot had clearly run through the croissant's chocolaty center.

"I love all creatures, and amphibians are no exception," Zelda said, a lone tear trickling down her face. "I am very dedicated to helping save them. But I don't like them cavorting in my food."

"Understandably so," said the reporter, shaking her head.

"I feel so traumatized!" Zelda added for emphasis.

Once again, Bree couldn't help but stare at the television in disbelief.

Since when did Zelda love salamanders? Since when did Zelda love anything? And how had the salamanders gotten into the patisserie, anyway? It's not like they were velociraptors with opposable-thumb-claws that could open doors. They were tiny little amphibians who could barely make it across the street.

Also, since when did Zelda cry? The only time Bree had ever seen her exhibit any emotion was that day in her mom's closet, and even then she had just been acting to get everyone in trouble.

And that's when it occurred to her: What if Zelda was acting again? What if this was all some sort of performance, and she was manipulating the situation to get whatever it was she wanted? But why would she do that? Was this just another one of her pranks, where this time the joke was on the local news and the entire town? It didn't make sense.

"After all the work Bree Robinson has done to save the salamanders," said Zelda, looking directly into the camera, "it breaks my heart that this shop would put the salamander population in danger by letting them run rampant in their kitchen. Salamanders shouldn't be trusted near open flames! They belong in the wild. And now the Board of Health will want to get involved and—"

"Hold on a moment," the reported interrupted. "I thought it was that hyper-responsible Twiggs girl who's saving the salamanders."

"No!" Zelda cried, emphatically. "Everyone got that wrong. The movement was started by a girl named Bree Robinson and then Chelsea stepped in and took all the credit. But Bree did it all, including planning this huge fund-raiser, taking place this Saturday at Playa del Mar Middle School. Everyone should go!"

What on earth was going on here?

Zelda looked straight into the camera like a salesperson in an infomercial as she repeated, "Again, it's being held on the field at Playa del Mar Middle School, and the festivities start at noon. There will be games and food and crafts and things available for purchase. All are welcome!"

Bree's heart soared. She had no idea why any of this was happening, but her current biggest dream had just come true.

The fund-raiser had just been advertised on the local news, and the segment would likely get replayed over and over throughout the day. Zelda, the most unlikely champion, had just set the record straight *and* made a PR plug for the big Save the Salamanders fund-raiser.

Was it possible that Zelda had just happened to be at the patisserie when a salamander stepped on her *pain au chocolat*? But salamanders didn't even like chocolate! They much preferred insects.

Something just didn't add up.

And then, right on cue, Bree's phone lit up. It was a group text message. And it was from Zelda.

CHAPTER TWENTY-EIGHT

MALIA

Malia looked at her phone, where she saw something disturbing: a message from Zelda.

The text was addressed to all three babysitters.

I think we need to meet. I have a lot to tell you.

A moment later, Malia also received a message from her Venmo account, saying Zelda had sent her money. What? Zelda didn't owe her anything—she hadn't done any babysitting for them. Yet there it was, with a message: **Fee from babysitting Chase/Clark/Smith, minus my cut, of course.**

A moment later, her brow still furrowed in a look of utter confusion, Malia received a frantic phone call from Bree, saying Zelda had just appeared on the news.

"There was a lizard footprint in the chocolate center!" she

yelled. "On the news! I mean, a salamander footprint! In the *chocolat*! But salamanders don't like chocolate! And they can't open cabinets! And Zelda cried!" After a few minutes of yelling, it still didn't make a lot of sense. But whatever it was sounded urgent enough to warrant an emergency board meeting.

"I tried to get snacks for the occasion and the patisserie is closed!" Dot said, rushing up to the gazebo to meet her friends. "What is going on with the universe today?"

"You can't get pastries because there was a lizard footprint and it was on the news and I don't know what happened and that's what we're trying to figure out!" Bree exploded. Malia couldn't remember ever seeing her friend so anxious before.

"Something weird is going on," Malia said. "Zelda was on the news this morning, bad-mouthing the patisserie and telling everyone that Bree started Save the Salamanders. And she also sent me the fee from her last job with the boys, even though she didn't owe us."

"What?" asked Dot. "Do we think this is another prank?"

Malia shrugged. "She should be here any minute. She can set the record straight."

Zelda sauntered up to the gazebo, wearing a green dress with tiny pink flowers printed on it. It reminded Malia ever so slightly of the dresses Zelda had worn back in preschool.

"Hi," Zelda said.

"What do you want?" Malia narrowed her eyes. She didn't have time for games.

"Do you really not know why I called you here?"

"I mean, I have an idea. But I'm not, like, psychic."

"Like the five-year-old boys think you are," said Dot.

"Touché," said Zelda. "So I supposed you want an explanation about what happened with the babysitting job."

"And the lizard footprint in the chocolate," Bree chimed in.

"And the local news," said Dot.

"Right, right." Zelda tented her fingers. "Okay, so this might come as sort of a surprise to you guys, but I haven't had the easiest time making friends."

"You don't say!" said Malia.

"Very funny." Zelda hesitated a moment. She bit her lip, as if she were nervous, but that couldn't be right, because evil people didn't get nervous. "Look, I feel like a little ridiculous for admitting this, but my mom didn't hire you because she felt sorry for you and your business. She actually called you because she thought it would be nice for me to spend some time with people my own age. You know, outside of school."

"You mean, like . . . friends?" said Malia.

Zelda shrugged. "Yeah. Of course, I thought it was the

dumbest, most insulting thing I'd ever heard. I mean, what kind of parent does such a thing? Trying to *buy* me friends? And what if anyone at school had heard about it? Like, that I needed babysitting by people my own age?"

Malia actually started to feel a little bad for Zelda. She imagined that couldn't be an easy situation for anyone, even someone as tough-seeming as Zelda.

"Anyway, I figured I'd better stay in control of the situation. Stay one step ahead of you guys, keep you so focused on how bad the situation was for *you* that you never realized how humiliating it was for *me*. But I wasn't prepared to actually enjoy hanging out with you guys."

"We enjoyed hanging out with you, too," Malia said. "That is, until you kept screwing us over."

"Yeah, I know. Old habits die hard, I guess. But a lot of things actually weren't my fault. Like, Dot, when you said all the weird things that day at the patisserie? It was only because the evil boys got control of my phone and started saying things about farts into the translator."

At the memory of the incident, Dot looked embarrassed all over again.

"And when Chase's mom called to hire me as their only sitter, I actually argued against it. I told her how we work as a team. But she was really set on this new plan, and I worried that if I didn't say yes, we might lose out on their business entirely. But I think with a little more time, I can convince her to let us all come back together."

"But what about the lizard footprint in the chocolate?!" Bree cut in. It was clear that she couldn't wait another second for the explanation.

"Well, that was totally my doing. I saw Chelsea on the news the other day, and how she took credit for your ideas. I may like to cause trouble, and I may be a pain a lot of the time, but I have no tolerance for people who try to take all the credit for things they didn't do. I couldn't just sit around and do nothing."

"So . . . what did you do?" Bree pressed.

"I staged the whole thing. I borrowed one salamander from the crossing and brought it to the bakery and had it step on my croissant."

Bree made a horrified face.

"Don't worry, it wasn't harmed. I returned it to the crosswalk afterward and it merrily went on its way."

Bree's face returned to normal.

"But did you hear? Jolie Pâtisserie is moving to Playa del Norte. I guess the Board of Health threatened to shut them down, and they're looking for a new start."

"All because of the lizard fiasco?" Malia couldn't believe her ears.

"Well, there was no lizard infestation, of course. I made that up. But the Board of Health needed to investigate, and when they checked out the kitchen, they found a whole bunch of other unsettling things back there. I just helped bring it all to light." Zelda seemed exceptionally pleased with herself.

"So, there will be no more delicious bread products?" Dot looked genuinely saddened by this. Though she hated the au pairs more than anyone, she was also the biggest fan of wheat-based baked goods.

"Well, yes, it means no more French pastries. But it also means no more French babysitters. Obviously, the au pairs are all moving to Playa del Norte as well, since they have no choice but to move along with their parents. So both businesses are leaving town."

This was the best news Malia had ever heard. It felt like a miracle had taken place. But it wasn't a miracle; it was Zelda.

Despite everything Zelda had put them through over the years, Malia found herself feeling sorry for Zelda. Maybe she kept acting out because she was lonely and misunderstood.

Zelda shifted her feet. "I guess this is my way of saying that I'm really sorry for the way I've treated you in the past. I know you can never forget some of the things I've done, and it might be hard to forgive my actions, but I hope you will."

No sooner had Malia started to process Zelda's apology than her cell phone started ringing. It was Mrs. Gregory.

"Malia? It's Mrs. Gregory. Oh, it is so good to hear your voice. I don't suppose you and the girls have any openings this week?"

"Oh! Why, yes, I think we do. Let me check the calendar!"

While Malia pretended to check their definitely empty calendar, another call came in on her call waiting. It was Wendy Blatt, Aloysius's mom. While Malia was taking that call, she received a text from Dina Larsson and a voicemail from the Woos, both requesting babysitting services. Malia made a note of all the jobs they already had on the calendar for the coming week. It was nearly more than they could handle, but she knew this was a good problem to have and she was determined to appreciate it.

Malia sat on the gazebo floor, trying to figure out how to cover all the jobs. Zelda sat down next to her, along with the others. It felt weird to have a fourth person there, in what had become their sacred space of friendship. But it also felt weird in a good way, like Zelda somehow belonged. That was when she realized that maybe the solution was right in front of her.

"Hey, Zelda, do you think maybe you could babysit the Gregory kids this Wednesday?"

Zelda gave her an almost shy smile and nodded. "Sure!"

The four girls chattered happily as they continued assigning jobs, their voices echoing through the gazebo, thrilled to be back to babysitting.

Business wasn't just back—it was booming. Thanks to the most unlikely of allies, peace had been restored. The nightmare was over.

CHAPTER TWENTY-NINE
Dot

For today's episode of *Trio of Doom*, Chase answered the door with his finger lodged in his nose.

"Hi there, Chase," said Dot. "Are you digging for treasure?"

"I'm collecting boogers to add to my collection," he said, as if this were an everyday occurrence. Which, for him, maybe it was.

"Oh," said Dot. "Is that sanitary?"

He shrugged. "I keep them in a box." Then he walked off into the house, finger still securely in his nostril.

As her final act of charity, Zelda had convinced Chase's mom to hire back the babysitters, and today, Zelda and Dot were tackling the job together. Dot supposed winning this job back wasn't as necessary now that the rest of their clients were once again in need of sitters, but it was a matter of pride. After suffering so very much at the hands of these devils, she needed to go out on a high note. And she was prepared. Today, the tide was going to turn. It was going to be great.

"MY NAME IS MONSIEUR BUTT!" yelled Smith as the girls entered the living room.

"Time for the Monsieur Butt dance!" said Clark.

Smith started singing a weird song that had no lyrics, just "dun dun dun dun dun," and all three boys broke out into a very spirited jig.

"Butt! Butt! Butt! Butt!" chanted Chase, shaking his rump.

"MONSIEUR BUTT SAYS, JUMP!" yelled Smith.

The other boys jumped.

"MONSIEUR BUTT SAYS, FREEZE!"

The other boys froze.

It appeared this was some sort of bizarre version of Simon Says.

"MONSIEUR BUTT SAYS, FART!"

All three boys let loose an epic fart. Then they collapsed on the ground in a fit of giggles.

"Okay, that is NOT mature." Dot crossed her arms.

"WE'RE FIVE!" Smith yelled.

This was a valid point.

Dot supposed there was no time like the present to share her secret plan with the boys.

"All right. We're going to play a game! But we have to do it in the yard!" Dot said, rounding them up and scooting them out the back door. They clambered across the deck, down the steps, and onto the grass, where Dot could enact her secret plan without making too much of a mess.

"REMEMBER WHEN YOU GOT SPRAYED BY THE SKUNKS?" Smith laughed.

"I do," Dot said.

"THAT WAS SO FUNNY!" Smith continued.

"Hahahahahahahahaha!" Clark dissolved into laughter.

"That was the grossest ever!" Chase agreed.

"Okay, so here is how we play the game." Dot was all business. "You line up in front of those bushes. And you stay very still like statues, and you close your eyes. And you don't open them until I say it's time."

"AND THEN WHAT HAPPENS?" Smith demanded.

"I can't tell you, because it's a surprise."

"I DON'T LIKE SURPRISES!"

"Yeah, we don't like surprises," Chase chimed in.

"I promise it's worth it," Zelda added.

The boys considered this for a second. Having received the witch's encouragement, they reluctantly lined up and closed their eyes.

As soon as the boys weren't looking, Dot and Zelda retrieved the Super Soakers they had hidden near the deck upon their arrival. They were filled with a special slime Dot had developed in the science lab: an ooey-gooey jelly formula—green, sticky, gross. Dot made sure that it was machine-washable and, of course, nontoxic.

"Ready?" Dot asked. "The surprise is coming, but you can't open your eyes until I say so."

They looked at one another, silently counting backward from three.

Then she and Zelda sprayed the contents of the Super Soakers all over the boys. They were immediately coated in a gooey neon-green liquid, like something out of a TV show.

"Aaaaaaaaaaaauuuuuuuuuugh!" yelled Clark.

"WHAT IS THIS? IS THIS SLIME?" yelled Smith, walking around with his arms extended, like a zombie.

Chase was just confused. He patted himself all over, trying to make sense of the strange mixture now coating his body.

"HOW DARE YOU ATTACK ME, VILE SITTER

WOMAN!" screamed an indignant Smith. "YOU SHALL NOT PREVAIL! I WILL RETALIATE WITH MY WIZARD SPELL!"

"What IS this stuff?" asked Chase, who honestly seemed more intrigued than annoyed.

"It's a lot like boogers, actually," said Dot. "In a minute, it's going to start to solidify. And you'll be trapped. Frozen in time, like a mummy."

This part was a little white lie, but she thought it would be funny to see them react.

"WHAT?" yelled Smith. "HOW IS THAT POSSIBLE?"

"My parents are going to be so mad," said Clark.

"Yeah! You'll never get away with this," said Chase.

"Not so. Your parents will never know the difference, because the slime washes off with water. Disappears without a trace." Dot smiled. "But I'm not letting you go until I decide that it's time. I call this game 'Human Statues.'"

Smith shot her a look of death.

Dot was very, very pleased with herself.

"You're even more powerful than a witch," said Chase.

"You're a wizard!" said Clark, who stood in a particularly amusing jumping-jack pose.

"CAN YOU TEACH ME HOW TO MAKE MY OWN SLIME?" asked Smith.

"Maybe one day. If you get on my good side," said Dot.

"I wanna learn, too!" said Chase.

"Me too!" Clark chimed in.

"THE WIZARD IS THE COOLEST BABYSITTER EVER!" Smith yelled, so loudly he was likely heard in outer space. And for once, Dot was happy about that.

CHAPTER THIRTY

Bree

Bree looked around and felt flooded with feelings. All her hard work had come down to this moment: the day of the Save the Salamanders Carnival Fund-Raiser Extravaganza. Before this moment, Bree had thought the rally in the gazebo was her proudest moment. Or the first time she helped a salamander safely cross the street. Or maybe that one time, which had happened five years ago and had nothing to do with saving anything. Regardless, none of those moments were her proudest moment, as it turned out. Because this was incredible.

Bree scanned the crowd gathered on the grounds of the Playa del Mar school. Families milled about. The soccer boys loitered beneath a giant tree. Chelsea, on the other hand, was nowhere to be seen. But Bree figured it was only a matter of time before she waltzed in and acted like the entire day had been her doing.

In honor of the occasion, Bree—well, technically Bree's mom—had convinced the school to let her take over not just the sports field, but also the entire property for the day. In the parking lot, a taco truck had already attracted a huge line of people. Encircling the field and the surrounding paths were big folding tables, where all sorts of donated items were being sold. Some of Bree's fellow students were selling baked goods, local parents were selling their crafts—ceramics, needlepoint, handmade jewelry—and Dot's mom was giving tarot readings. The school had even set up a podium at one end of the soccer field, which Bree, Dot, and Malia had decorated with green and brown and black balloons, the colors of a spotted salamander. The huge banner they had made read *SAVE THE SALAMANDERS!* in bold—but not glittery—letters.

Bree's very favorite part was the enormous inflatable dancing man, which the local used car dealership had donated for the day. The giant green form was visible for blocks and blocks and towered above them all, dancing in the wind. If you squinted, it almost looked like a joyful salamander.

Last but certainly not least, there was a giant bank—actually, a giant wooden box with a slot cut in the top, covered with cut-and-paste photos of salamanders—where people could put their donations. A number of people had already pledged coins and bills and even checks.

Bree had no idea how much money the carnival would raise. She had tried to figure it out, but she wasn't psychic, or particularly good at math. She could only hope for the best. But no matter how it all turned out, she couldn't help but feel proud of herself, and her friends, for putting it all together. The scene was truly impressive: bigger and more festive than she could have ever dreamed.

As Bree scanned the crowd, a huge black sports utility vehicle rolled up to the curb in the school parking lot. The license plate read *VER0NICA*, with a zero where the *O* should be.

WHAT?

No.

Could it be?

It was.

Bree gasped.

It was Veronica. The person, not the cat. Veronica had heard her cry. And she had answered it, in the most beautiful way.

Veronica emerged from the back seat, wearing an enormous silver puffer coat that went all the way down to her ankles. It didn't make a lot of sense, given the warm weather, but Bree thought it was the single most glamorous piece of clothing she had ever seen. On her feet, she wore high-heeled ankle booties in a corresponding silver glitter. They were so sparkly, it looked like they were covered with actual diamonds.

Bree felt like she was caught in one of those dreams where you tried to scream but no sound came out. She couldn't feel her face. She couldn't hear her thoughts. She couldn't make a sound. But she still felt AMAZING.

This was the most thrilling moment of Bree's entire life. She was so excited that she thought she might pee a little, but she managed to keep it under control. She knew that Veronica would never let her down! Veronica wasn't like Chelsea. She wasn't like all the other disappointing people in the world. Veronica cared. Veronica cared about people and Veronica cared about animals and—most incredibly of all—Veronica cared about Bree.

Already, a few people had noticed the presence of a pop star in their midst. It was only a matter of time before the rest of the crowd totally lost control.

Veronica strode across the school parking lot—their school parking lot!—accompanied by two other humans: a very serious-looking woman wearing super-pointy black shoes, a black suit, and a fedora; along with a giant man wearing a yellow sweat suit. He was the size of three men added together. Bree recognized him as the bodyguard Veronica was frequently photographed with.

"VERONICAAAAAAAA!" yelled Bree, the moment her sparkly heel hit the ground. She took off running, sprinting toward the parking lot. She had no idea what she was going to do when she got there. Was it okay to hug Veronica? Was it okay to cry tears of joy onto the shoulder of her puffer coat? Bree hoped she didn't look like a freak, but she was sure this sort of thing must happen to Veronica all the time.

"THANK YOU FOR ANSWERING MY NOTE!" Bree called.

But instead of recognition, Veronica looked at her with a mix of confusion and terror.

"IT'S ME, BREE!" she yelled.

Still nothing.

"I'm the one who named my cat after you," she said, quieter this time, since she had finally reached them.

Veronica turned to the serious suit lady for help.

"This is the girl," the suit lady said, angling her head at Bree.

"Ohhhh!" said Veronica, very quietly. She offered Bree a huge thumbs up and then clapped her hands.

"I'm Becky, Veronica's manager," the suit lady said, extending a hand. "Thank you so much for inviting Veronica to participate in this event. As an animal activist, she's so thrilled to be here."

Veronica nodded very enthusiastically.

"Veronica can't speak much, because she's resting her voice before the performance," Becky explained, reading Bree's expression. "But I can assure you that she's very glad to be here. Also, I have to insist that Veronica can perform only two songs today. We have music at the ready, but she's traveling without her backup dancers, so it will be a very pared-down version of the usual show."

"Oh! That's fine," said Bree. "Anything she does is more than perfect."

Becky nodded once. She acted more like a robot than a human. "All right. Let's get this show rolling, then, shall we?"

The bodyguard put one hand protectively on Veronica's back. "Which way to the stage?" he said, in an impossibly deep voice.

Bree pointed at the little raised platform at the end of the soccer field. Becky turned on one heel and began walking purposefully down the field, with the rest of Team Veronica close behind her.

Veronica paused at the side of the stage, while a member of her entourage checked to make sure the microphone was functioning. "Sound check! One, two, one, two! Check!" The microphone was, indeed, working. The show was about to begin.

As Veronica stepped up to the mike, the crowd surged and swarmed around the stage, growing ever larger. The excitement (and also the confusion) was palpable. Shrieks and screams rang out through the air, and a couple of students even fainted. Was Veronica really live in their small town? And at their school, no less?

The whole scene was easily one of the strangest things Bree had ever seen — Veronica, live, in Playa del Mar. And it was all because of her.

Malia looked amazed as she patted Bree on the back. "Well, kid, you've really done it. This is unlike anything that's ever happened at this school. Maybe in this town."

"Um, hi, Playa del Mar," said Veronica, speaking into the microphone. She pronounced it "Playa del Mare," but that was okay. She was Veronica, and she could do whatever she wanted. "I'm excited to be here today. We're about to sing about some lizards. But before we get down to it, I want to give a very special shout-out to the girl who named her cat after me."

Bree nearly fainted.

"Without her, I wouldn't be here today and, like, neither would the lizards. So thank you for caring, Bree."

A cheer went up from the crowd.

The music came blaring from the speakers that lined the field. It was the single "Selfie to my Soul," but as Veronica started singing, it became clear that this was a special version. A *very* special version, unlike anything that had ever been recorded.

"*Seflie-selfie-selfie-mander,*" Veronica sang. "*You're the lizard of my heart.*"

"Did she just say 'selfie-mander'?" Dot looked horrified. "WHAT is a selfie-mander?"

"Maybe it's, like, a selfie you take, while holding a salamander," Bree explained.

"This song doesn't really make sense," Malia confirmed.

"*Sala-sala-mander-mander, love whenever we're together. Sort of pretty, sort of slimy, in the dirt so grimy-grimy.*"

"I think she's making it up as she goes along." Dot shook her head.

Indeed, it seemed like Veronica was singing in a language

all her own. And it was magnificent. She had shown up, and that alone was incredible. Seeing her getting in the spirit in this way was more than Bree had ever dreamed of. All around, everyone was dancing, caught up in the fever of Veronica, live, in Playa del Mar. She had never seen her peers so excited about anything as they were right now, about Veronica. (And also about salamanders, obvi.)

"It's beautiful," said Bree. Because it was.

By the end of Veronica's performance, the makeshift lizard bank was overflowing with donations, and a line of people had formed to add even more. Bree didn't even have to count them to know they had more than they needed to build the salamanders a bridge to the future.

Now there was just one thing left to attend to.

Chelsea, dressed in jeans and a white eyelet top, meandered slowly over to the group.

"This is quite a turnout!" she said. "It seriously might be the most exciting thing that's ever happened on school property." She seemed happy, maybe even a little bit proud, of the surrounding event. Bree was confused. Did Chelsea actually think she was responsible for it? Did she just not care?

"I can't believe you had the nerve to show up here," spat Malia.

"I suppose you're going to try to take credit for this, too?" Dot asked.

With her friends there for backup, Bree knew it was time to speak up. "You know, I was really upset with what you did," she said, looking Chelsea in her huge brown eyes. "Not just because I thought you were better than that. But because I thought you cared about the salamanders."

Chelsea looked wounded.

"I don't need anyone to think I'm a hero," Bree continued. "I don't care about anyone getting credit, whether it's me or not. But I can't believe that you would go out of your way to get the glory when there is something as serious as animal welfare at stake!"

She expected Chelsea to argue with her, or counter her with a lot of words Bree didn't understand. But all she said was, "You're right." Bree was shocked.

"Of COURSE she's right," Malia scoffed.

"You know that I'm really, really lucky. I'm great at school, I excel at extracurriculars, I'm likely going to have my choice of whatever college I want," Chelsea continued. "But if I'm being honest, I've always been sort of jealous of what you guys have."

"What do you mean?" Bree asked.

"Not your business, per se. I mean, when I started the Seaside Sitters, we took over all your business in about five minutes."

"Oh my god, Chelsea, do not get me started." Malia held up her hands in a sign of disgust.

"My point is more like, you guys are so . . . *close*."

"I mean, yeah, because we're best friends," said Malia.

"Yes, I know, and I have friends, too, obviously." Chelsea rolled her eyes. "I just admire how you guys go after things because you really care about them. You go after things you're passionate about, and that is a rare quality."

"Thank you," Bree said.

Bree couldn't help but feel a little bit bad for Chelsea. She was still kind of slimy, and definitely not to be trusted, but she had done some good after all. She had reminded Bree just how wonderful her friendships were.

"Also, Veronica totally saved the day!" said Chelsea. "That's a bigger name than even Ramona could guarantee." Bree beamed. But just when Bree thought that Chelsea had shown her goodness, Chelsea opened her mouth again. "I mean, what were the odds of that? Total luck!" Chelsea said, with a sinister laugh. Then she turned and walked off.

"Well," said Malia. "Some things never change."

"That's true," said Bree. "But at least other things do."

Bree looked around at the scene unfolding on the field—the people, the magic, and the money they had raised. It all felt a little bittersweet. Once the bridge was done, her work here would be done as well. The salamanders wouldn't need her to usher them to safety. But she would know that she had made a difference. And her work, like her memories of this day, would live on.

CHAPTER THIRTY-ONE

MALIA

Once again, Malia found herself reflecting on the nature of change. Sometimes, things could change dramatically, seemingly overnight. In a short amount of time, their business had all but disappeared, and then everything had righted itself—thanks to Zelda—in a matter of days.

Other times, Malia thought, checking her phone for what must have been the bazillionth time, barely anything changed. Connor Kelly still hadn't texted her. She was starting to accept that he never would.

"Is everything okay?" Bree asked.

"Yeah! Does it seem like something is wrong?" Malia said unconvincingly.

"You just keep looking at your phone."

"Oh! I'm just checking my notes before the ceremony,"

Malia lied. It wasn't that she wasn't comfortable sharing her rejection with her friend. Her ego simply wouldn't let her speak the words. For now, the best she could do was to focus on the task at hand: Zelda's official hiring ceremony.

Not only had Zelda become their friend, she was becoming the fourth member of Best Babysitters. It was the least they could do after Zelda had single-handedly solved the French au pair problem and proven herself the most gifted babysitter the world had ever known. No one could anticipate a prank better than Zelda, and she commanded respect from pretty much everyone she encountered.

"Since we couldn't get *pain au chocolat* for the occasion, I made cupcakes!" Bree exclaimed, taking a large piece of aluminum foil off a giant cupcake tray. In typical Bree fashion, the cupcakes were absolutely covered in colorful rainbow sprinkles. They appeared to be more sprinkle than cupcake.

"Wow!" said Dot, then added, "Are you sure that much decoration is edible?"

"I'm honored," said Zelda.

"And we are thrilled to have you!" said Malia. "On this momentous occasion, I'd like to give a little speech." She cleared her throat and looked at the notes she'd prepared on her phone. "I've been thinking a lot about destiny."

"Oh boy," groaned Dot.

"Or rather, I've been thinking about how destiny is something we create for ourselves." Malia used to be a big believer in fate. There were certain moments — like meeting her friends, or getting the idea to form Best Babysitters — that felt meant to be. But now, after nothing had happened with Connor, she was starting to change her tune. "I admire you, Zelda, for the way you've so obviously taken fate into your own hands over these past few weeks. Over the years, you've really proven yourself to be a person who, uh, makes things happen. And now that you're focusing on making *good* things happen, well, I don't think anyone will be able to stop you. You are truly a force to be reckoned with. So congratulations! And welcome aboard."

The girls each plucked a sprinkle-covered cupcake from the tray and held them up to one another's like champagne glasses.

"I can't believe I'm sitting here with you guys cheers-ing with cupcakes like a bunch of tryhards," said Zelda. "But I mean that in the best way possible."

It was the truth, thought Malia. Who would have thought that Zelda — the world's weirdest babysitting charge — would have made such a wonderful sitter herself? But if seventh grade had taught Malia anything so far, it was that the world was full of surprises.

There was no better moment for a surprise to pop up on Malia's phone.

When she saw what it said, she screamed a little. It was a name that had never appeared on her screen before: *Connor.*

Malia practically hyperventilated. Connor Kelly had remembered that her number lived in his phone, and then —miracle of miracles—he had actually used it. Her friends looked at her quizzically. Malia held up her phone, where the lone message was beckoning her to read it.

"Oh my goodness!" said Bree.

"Whoa. You guys are moving to actual technological communications?" said Dot. "I thought I'd never see the day."

"So? What did he say?" asked Zelda.

"What do I do?" Malia said.

"Read it!" Zelda commanded.

Malia opened the message, fingers trembling. She suddenly grew nervous. What if he had sent her a message by accident? What if it was actually a group text? What if he was just asking her to clarify a homework assignment or something?

But when she opened the message, she was relieved to see it was just for her, and it was everything she'd ever hoped for.

Hey.

It was absolutely perfect.

Hey, Malia wrote back.

In a world full of complications, sometimes the simple things really were the best.